## "Look in th[e mirror.]
## You're a beautiful woman."

Rob turned the lamp on the bedside table up higher, and mesmerized by his commanding voice, Laura did as she was told. Then she gasped as his hands moved caressingly over her body. There was a buzzing in her ears and her internal controls had all disintegrated.

Suddenly all her alarm bells went off. She clutched at his wandering hands.

"What are you doing to me?" she whispered.

Rob laughed and gently kissed her neck. "What are you *letting* me do?" he replied. And then he turned and left. Moments later she heard the sound of his jeep rattling up the hill.

For the rest of the night she tossed and turned, trying to find the answer to his question. He was right. She had *let* him do it. Worse, she had almost begged for it. . . .

**Emma Goldrick** describes herself as a grandmother first and an author second. She was born and raised in Puerto Rico, where she met her husband, a career military man from Massachusetts. His postings took them all over the world, which often led to mishaps—such as the Christmas they arrived in Germany before their furniture. Emma uses the places she's been as backgrounds for her books, but just in case she runs short of settings, this prolific author and her husband are always making new travel plans.

## Books by Emma Goldrick

### HARLEQUIN ROMANCE

2661—THE ROAD
2739—THE TROUBLE WITH BRIDGES
2846—TEMPERED BY FIRE
2858—KING OF THE HILL
2889—TEMPORARY PARAGON

### HARLEQUIN PRESENTS

688—AND BLOW YOUR HOUSE DOWN
791—MISS MARY'S HUSBAND
825—NIGHT BELLS BLOOMING
841—RENT-A-BRIDE LTD.
866—DAUGHTER OF THE SEA
890—THE OVER-MOUNTAIN MAN
953—HIDDEN TREASURES
1035—IF LOVE BE BLIND
1087—MY BROTHER'S KEEPER

Don't miss any of our special offers. Write to us at the following address for information on our newest releases.

Harlequin Reader Service
901 Fuhrmann Blvd., P.O. Box 1397, Buffalo, NY 14240
Canadian address: P.O. Box 603,
Fort Erie, Ont. L2A 5X3

# To Tame a Tycoon

**Emma Goldrick**

# Harlequin Books

TORONTO • NEW YORK • LONDON
AMSTERDAM • PARIS • SYDNEY • HAMBURG
STOCKHOLM • ATHENS • TOKYO • MILAN

Original hardcover edition published in 1988
by Mills & Boon Limited

ISBN 0-373-02943-8

Harlequin Romance first edition November 1988

To Doctor Michael Joseph Norton III, DMD
who inadvertently became my
Technical Advisor

# CHAPTER ONE

IT WAS a dark winter morning as New York lay in the grip of a north-westerly wind, and huge raindrops pelted the narrow canyons of the financial district. Forecasters were describing worse things to come from the plains of Canada. When the elevator stopped at the thirty-eighth floor and Robert Carlton came out into the lobby, things took on a brighter hue, at least for the women workers within sight. He gave them all a quick smile, dropped a quip off at the reception desk, and went on scattering sunshine, into the inner offices of Carltonworld, Toymakers.

'It's not something he does intentionally,' the receptionist explained to her new apprentice. 'It just happens. You should see when he *really* turns it on!' They both stared after him. Six feet of masculinity. Jet-black hair, with a tiny peppering of white, acknowledging his thirty-two years. A broad forehead, slimming down to a narrow jutting chin were separated by wide brown eyes, so dark as to be almost black. He carried his one hundred and eighty pounds, cased in a three-piece dark grey suit, lightly and with a sparkle.

'Twenty-five minutes,' his secretary told him. He gave her a smile for a thank-you. For all her forty-five years and rotund figure, she felt the jolt of him, and wished for a moment that she was younger, or her eldest daughter a little older.

'Are the vultures waiting?' A nice baritone voice he had. *Maybe he has too much*, Mrs Saitemore thought.

'They've been gathered for the past half-hour.'

7

Robert winked an eye at the tone of her reproof. 'That's what they get paid for, Mary. Send in some coffee? I managed to get home late—or early—and missed breakfast.'

'I understand. Now you've only twenty minutes before you must leave for the airport.'

'Why did I ever buy a watch when I have you on hand, Mary? All right, I'm going!'

He glided into the other office; it was the way of him. He moved like some lithe jungle animal, without sound, without visible exertion. The two men waiting got to their feet as he went around behind the desk. He took a moment to stand at the executive window. There was a view, as city views go, with the twin towers of the World Trade building settled in the centre of it. He stretched tired muscles, and turned around.

'Henry?'

Henry Weggins, prematurely bald, perspiring in the air-conditioned room, swallowed hard. 'The—er—deal has come unstuck,' he reported nervously. 'Her lawyer hasn't returned the signed proxies.'

'You tried a little leverage on him?'

'Hardly, sir. I am informed by our enquiry agents in Hartford——' Henry waved a Telex form in the air between them as a defensive measure. 'They inform me—us—that Mr Ladessy, the lawyer representing Miss E. Lackland, is no longer in business.'

'Well, find him and get him back *in* business!' For just a moment Robert's control slipped, and they felt the bite of wrath in his voice.

'We *did* find him,' Henry Weggins complained, shaken by the crunch, but still holding his own. 'In the Cedars of Mercy cemetery outside Hartford, Connecticut. It seems that Mr Ladessy died perhaps three months ago.'

'I told you not to put faith in a lawyer of Hungarian ancestry.' The second man in the room smiled cheerlessly.

'Oh, shut up, Harry,' Robert Carlton snapped. 'Just because you're my brother-in-law it doesn't mean you can never be made redundant.'

'But your sister would be rather angry, don't you think?'

'I might be willing to risk that chance,' Robert Carlton returned. The restlessness was returning again; it had haunted him too many times in the past month. He had played the tycoon for so many years now that the *real* Rob Carlton could hardly escape. Just for one moment he felt like throwing the whole thing up, but there were too many responsibilities. He banged one closed fist into the other and stared at his brother-in-law.

'Review the situation for me.'

'Very well. You've proposed, as chief executive officer, that we suspend all sales and productions on our Little Mother line of dolls, which happen to be our biggest sellers. The remaining members of the board not only condemn this policy, but also intend to vote for your dismissal from the executive post.'

'As they've been trying to do on every issue for the past seven years,' Robert Carlton said bitterly. 'Although they're all willing to spend the millions we've made on my risk-takings over the past seven years, they're not prepared to accept a loss. They all know now that we should never have put Little Mother on the market. It's dangerous. We know it, and the Federal Government knows it. All we can do is cut out losses, shut down, redesign, and try again later.'

'Yes, well...' Robert's brother-in-law was a waffler of great renown. He meant to come down on the winning side, whatever that side might be. 'At the moment you hold approximately forty per cent of the stock. The other directors, and your sister, hold forty-five per cent.'

'And this E. Lackland owns the rest?'

'Yes. Miss Lackland inherits from her grandmother, your own father's partner.'

'You're intimating that my own sister is prepared to vote against me?' That silky-soft voice, with the subtle threat behind it.

Harry Marks held up his hands, palms forward. 'I didn't *say* that,' he responded.

'But she does what you tell her to, doesn't she, Harry?' Harry shrugged his shoulders.

'So, what can we do about all this?'

'Compromise,' Harry interjected hurriedly. 'Don't write off the programme. Do suspend the sales in the United States, but push them in the overseas markets. We need that income.'

'Of course we do,' Robert said coldly. 'We'll dump every blemish and poison that we make into the overseas market. After all, what do they know! All right, that's enough for now—I have a trip to make. Both of you get back to work.'

His secretary came into the office as the men left. He turned to the coat rack, shaking his head. She helped him with one sleeve. 'You know the answer,' she told him softly. 'You can't let them steal the corporation that *you* built. It almost went bankrupt under their hands after your father died.'

'If I know that answer, it seems to have escaped me,' he grumbled. 'Are all the papers for the Illinois factory inspection available? You know, Mary, sometimes I wonder if this is all worth the chase. I could just as easily be back in some small university, teaching electronics.'

'In your briefcase, along with some samples. And you *know* you couldn't give up the chase under a cloud.'

'All right, Office Mother,' he chuckled, 'explain it. What could I do to answer the problem, even though I can't think of a thing? In very simple terms, of course.'

Mrs Saitemore opened the shorthand pad that accompanied her everywhere. 'Miss Emerald Lackland,' she read. 'American by birth, although we know nothing about the time and place and circumstances. She would be the daughter of the only son of Jacob Blake, your father's life partner. We actually know nothing about her. Her grandfather died at sixty-eight. Following the rule-of-thumb on generations, his son would have been about forty-eight at the time, and we might conclude that the daughter is about twenty-eight. Her mother was a model, so I presume that makes the granddaughter a beautiful woman.'

'That's not a great deal to know about a girl who holds fifteen per cent of our stock. Where does she live?'

'We have a mail address: Miss Emerald Lackland, Lower Hell's Gate, Saba, Dutch Antilles.'

'Good lord, I've never heard of the place! In the Caribbean somewhere?'

'Somewhere. And all you have to do is find her, and give her one of those big smiles.'

'Why, Mary Saitemore, you *are* a romantic, aren't you?' Robert laughed down at her, but there was a look of puzzlement in the depths of those dark eyes. He pondered, then let the smile slip away.

'It's worth it,' Mary cautioned.

'Probably,' he sighed. 'But I never thought I'd come to prostitution, hiring myself out as a stud like that!'

'Mr Carlton! What a thing to say!'

The smile came back to his face. He tipped up his secretary's chin with a strong mid-finger and kissed her lightly on the forehead before he headed for the elevator.

The rain became a downpour before they reached Kennedy Airport. Robert's liaison man met him at the concourse and escorted him to the VIP lounge. 'Everything is set, Mr Carlton,' he said nervously. His very nervousness annoyed Robert Carlton. Everywhere he turned these days, people were bowing and scraping, and it irritated. As did the solid sheet of rain beating at the windows of the airport terminal building. In fact, he told himself, the whole damn world irritates me. What I need is something different; something important to dig into. If the board of directors were to meet right here in this lobby and vote me out—I'd be glad. Damn glad!

'Sir?' The young man was tugging at his sleeve. 'Your flight to Chicago boards in fifteen minutes, and we should be moving to the gate now.'

'How far is it to Saba?'

'Where?' The American was a taller and slimmer model of Henry Weggins. He was prepared to talk about finances and manufacturing, but Saba was a name beyond his comprehension.

*And beyond mine, too, an hour ago,* Rob Carlton told himself. But a tycoon never lets ordinary men see that he's only human, after all. The idea brought a wry smile to his face. 'Saba,' he prodded. 'An island in the Dutch Antilles.'

'I don't know, Mr Carlton. I never heard of it before.'

'But you can get me a seat on a flight going that far?'

'I'm sure I could,' the young man half promised. 'For tomorrow?'

'For some time in the next half-hour!'

'But—but the appointment in Chicago? You know that this independent Illinois factory is producing at a rate of almost twenty per cent better than our own three facilities. We need not only their output but also their know-how. That plant is worth millions—and three of our competitors are already putting out feelers!'

And you won't earn your ten per cent commission and finder's fee, thought Robert. Poor man. 'Thank you for your lecture in management,' he said gently. 'I don't feel like buying a factory today. I *do* feel like flying south into the sun. Well?'

The young man almost choked over his apology, and rushed off to one of the counters. It proved to be easier than expected. There were always empty first-class seats, and Rob Carlton was in one of them when the 747 jumbo splashed down the runway and headed south. They flew into the sunshine almost immediately, thirty thousand feet high above the Atlantic flight corridor. Usually, Robert slept on long flights, his mind able to shut down his body at a moment's notice. But not this time. He had committed himself, deviated from the approved corporate course, off into the wild blue. He chuckled at that. He hadn't felt this—young—since his last university vacation, when he had taken his twenty-foot sloop out into the Atlantic and cruised the South Atlantic for no good purpose at all.

He loosened his tie and ordered a drink. Two stewardesses hurried to help. He rewarded them both with a smile, and they went back down the aisle feeling well paid. The sun continued to shine when they landed at the International Airport in San Juan, where he transferred to a smaller craft for the island-hop to French St Martin. Or Dutch Sint Maarten, depending on which half of the divided island one happened to like. The itch, the excitement, the feeling that he had his foot through a half-opened door, hung with him.

But getting from Sint Maarten to Saba was a different matter altogether. 'Saba?' the man at the flight desk repeated. 'Well, certainly you can fly to Saba—twice a week. Today is Friday, I could put you on the plane next Tuesday.'

Rob was tired. Flying was an exhausting business for passengers as well as crew, and the new force that was driving him just would not tolerate a delay. 'Damn it, ma    I can't wait that long. There has to be something sooner!'

'Helicopter! There is a helicopter service here. They might possibly charter a flight. Expensive, though. Would you wish me to call them?'

'Dear God, yes,' he groaned. 'Call them. I'll buy their aircraft if I have to!' The urge, the drive, was almost at panic-level now. He had come this far on a whim, but now he was chasing a dream, and he dared not let go. He had to find the woman, and get her proxy votes! He *had* to see her.

'Tomorrow?' the desk clerk asked him, telephone in hand. 'They could put you on a special flight tomorrow.'

'Today. How about in one hour, today?' The desk clerk looked at him, puzzled. Who in their right mind would want to hurry that much to get to Saba? Saba, the island that time had bypassed. The only island in the Caribbean with *no* sunny beaches. No beaches of any kind, for that matter. He muttered into the phone again, and then, 'He says he can do it, but it will cost a great deal.'

Rob slapped his open palm down hard on the wooden counter. 'Do it,' he ordered. The slapping sound cut across the chatter of this typically small passenger terminal. Everyone in the room turned to stare at him, and for a moment there was silence. He could feel the tropical Caribbean heat smash in on him. There was a tickle of smoke in his nose; someone was burning a canefield nearby. He shrugged himself out of his jacket, unbuttoned his shirt collar, and pulled his necktie down.

The helicopter made its appearance almost an hour later. It looked like one of those machines from the Korean war—one that had been on the losing side—but despite its rattles and shakes and groans it flew. Within minutes they were off, flying south-westward, into the afternoon glitter of the blue Caribbean.

'Is only a twenty-eight-mile flight. Where you go on Saba?' the pilot yelled as the overhead blades carved a path over the unmarked sea. Rob fumbled in his pocket for the slip of paper his secretary had thrust at him in New York. He felt uneasy. He was a long way from the seats of power.

'Lower Hell's Gate,' he read. 'Does that sound right?'

'Sure does. Right near the airport. You won't have to walk very far to reach it.'

'Walk?'

''Well, there's no flight due today, so the taxi won't be at the field, unless somebody comes down for something else, I don't think you'll find a soul at the airport. You want I should radio ahead for the taxi?'

'One? One taxi? My God, is this the end of the world?'

'Not exactly the end,' the pilot laughed. 'They got two taxis, but sometimes, you know, things don't run right. Plenty of people living on Saba, man—almost a thousand. Two or three islands, they so bad nobody lives there, but plenty people on Saba. You want I should radio?'

'So radio,' shrugged Rob, sinking down deeper into his seat.

'I radio. Maybe he comes.'

'Maybe?'

'Well, if he is not busy, you understand. Not to worry. You a big man. It's only six, maybe seven hundred feet up the mountain to Lower Hell. You make it easy. Nice day for walking, good breeze. Always a good breeze on Saba.'

Rob found out just what the pilot meant when the mountain top of Saba came poking up at them. It rose straight out of the depths of the ocean, a rounded peak whose shoulder and tangled crater marked it as an extinct volcano. He could see the red roofs of houses scattered in clusters along that shoulder, and gathered in a small heap within the crater.

The airport was a single runway at the lowest flat point on the island, a hundred feet or more above the water. The tarmac began at the cliffs on one side, and ran to the cliffs on the other, with both ends hanging out over the hundred-foot drop to the water. The pilot wrestled his light aircraft against the wind, and finally wheeled them to a stop. There were no buildings, but as they taxied down the runway they came to a large aircraft parking area. Rob leaned forward to peer out of the windows. An open jeep with a high canvas top in bright yellow, like the awning over an old grocery store, was coming down the snakelike road at high speed.

Rob climbed stiffly out of the helicopter, handing the pilot an extra ten dollars for his trouble, and made his way towards the dilapidated jeep. The engine of the helicopter roared, amplifying the strong breeze that was already trying to blow Rob away. He turned to watch as the machine staggered slowly up into the air, seemingly moving backwards under the wind pressure, and then zoomed away.

'Taxi?' he asked. The olive-skinned driver gave him a big smile and the gold tooth in the centre of his mouth flashed in the late afternoon sun. The man said something in Dutch, and Rob shook his head, not understanding a word of it.

'Lower Hell's Gate?' Rob added. The driver nodded again, and waited. Rob looked down at the scrap of paper again. There was no street address, and he wasn't sure just what the driver would require.

'Lackland?' he prodded. 'Miss Lackland?' The driver thought for a moment, then shook his head. Despite the breeze, the heat was getting to Rob now, punishing him for wearing his wool suit out of wintertime New York.

He dropped bag and jacket on the tarmac and shrugged himself out of his waistcoat.

'Miss Emerald Lackland?' he offered. The huge grin was displayed on the olive face again.

'Yes,' the driver encouraged. 'Miss Emerald.' He patted the seat of the jeep. 'Lower Hell's Gate, Miss Emerald.' They went up the hill like the Teddy Roosevelt charging up San Juan hill. The road zigged and zagged, and at high speed Rob's stomach felt queasy. They passed three or four scattered houses, white reinforced cement with red tile roofs. 'Lower Hell's Gate,' the driver said, pointing.

'That's *all* of it?'

The driver made no answer, but put his foot down on the gas pedal, and then, coming around a double curve, slammed on his brakes. 'Miss Emerald,' he said, pointing to the left and downward, to where a house nestled against the side of the mountain several feet below the road. A driveway curved downward towards it. Rob climbed out of the jeep, happy to find the ground was firm. How to pay? His fingers clutched at a variety of coins in different denominations from different countries. He brought them out and offered them in his open palm, and his driver laughed and made a judicious selection from among the American coins. Rob picked up his mass of coats, bags and briefcase, and started down the hill.

The walk was pleasant. Here, high on the mountain, the breeze was gentle, constant and cool. *But what am I doing here?* The thought brought him to a stop. By this time I should be stretching out in a luxury hotel room in Chicago with a glass of something cold in my hand. Real Kentucky bourbon, perhaps—I haven't tasted that in years. *So what am I doing here?* It isn't just the proxies, although that's important. It's more than that. A challenge, I suppose. Who the devil is this Miss

Emerald—this beauty about whom we know nothing? Jacob's granddaughter? The grandfather so outshone his family, I don't even remember his wife—or his son, for that matter. A terrible businessman, one of the major reasons why my father just could not rescue the company. Isn't that one for the book! I've come thousands of miles ou ·f my way to see if my intuition is playing me false. I could have had any of a hundred women in Chicago tonight, but I detoured all this distance just to be sure I wasn't missing out on a ripe plum, one who might just suit my fancy and save my company, all at the same time. Good lord, Carlton, you're really taking a flyer on *this* one!

The house was another white concrete building with the red-tiled roof he had seen everywhere. There evidently was only one style of architecture on Saba. It was low, built in a ranch style, curving around the shoulder of the hill, shaded by a cluster of palm trees. Things were quiet here at the front, and the sun had gone behind the peak of the mountain, leaving a cool, dry shade. From behind the house he could hear shouts of glee, a splash of water. Swimming pool? He smiled at his own deductions, rubbed a hand across his face, and knocked.

He could hear the footsteps coming, a slap-slap-slap that denoted loose slippers. For some reason his palms felt wet, and he rubbed them quickly on his jacket. She *has* to be here, he told himself. She *has* to! The screen door opened. A plump, cheerful, dark-skinned woman stood there, and he could just not find the words.

'Yes?' the woman said. There was the trace of some sort of accent, but he could not place it.

'Miss Emerald?' he asked.

'Yes?' The woman looked at him curiously, as if he were some kind of bug crawling out from beneath a wet rock.

'I've come from New York to see Miss Emerald,' he managed, feeling like a schoolboy in trouble. The woman frowned at him.

'You really mean that? You wanna see Miss Emerald?'

Rob cleared his throat. This is pure stupidity, he told himself, standing here arguing with a servant. And acting like a kid fresh out of college.

'Yes. I have some urgent business to transact with Miss Emerald.'

'Well, I don't know. Miss Emerald, she don't have nothing to do with no business, man. All the way from New York?'

'All the way.'

'I ain't sure, Mr——'

'Carlton,' he offered. 'Robert Carlton.'

'I ain't too sure, Mr Carlton, but why don't you come in and I'll see what Missy got to say?'

He followed her in, closing the screen door behind him. They were in a narrow hall, which led clear through the house to what must have been a back door. The woman gestured him into the first door on the right, and he walked in.

The transformation surprised him. He came out of a dark hall into a room flooded with light. Windows on all three sides were shaded by thin-slatted Venetian blinds. Paintings hung on every wall. Bamboo furniture, two or three comfortable chairs, a large sofa, and several pouffes, were scattered across a highly polished and tessellated wooden floor. There was a taste of Victorian upper-class about the whole affair.

'You wait here, Mr——'

'Carlton,' he repeated. 'Robert Carlton.'

From the back of the house he could hear the chatter of children come to an end. The woman cocked her head and smiled at him. 'Sound like they finished,' she said. 'Sit you down.'

She walked rapidly out of the room. Rather than sit, Rob looked around. There was a large painting hanging just opposite him. From that distance it looked like an example of the vague strokes from the Neo-Impressionist school. A young woman dressed in white stood at the edge of a cliff, looking at a man dressed sombrely in black. Rob walked over to examine it more closely. At a distance of about four feet everything in the picture seemed to change focus. He went closer. The man, the woman, the cliff, all were there in exquisite detail, but at this range he could see the look of fear on the woman's face, and the dark rage on the man's. The simple love scene had become a portrait of haunting murder. Rob shook his head to break away from the trance the picture had induced in him.

He backed away until his legs bumped into one of the chairs. His jacket, waistcoat, briefcase, were all dumped on the floor. The chair welcomed him. He sat there for what seemed to be an endless time, searching each of the other pictures, not daring to go near them. They were signed—'LaLa'—with a little scrawl at the bottom right corner.

'It must be jet-lag,' he muttered. A floorboard squeaked by the door and he looked over in that direction. A slender woman, dressed in shorts and T-shirt, the whole carelessly covered by an unbuttoned long white coat, strode into the room, brushing at her hands with a ball of cotton that smelled like turpentine. Her head was bent, examining the hand she was ruthlessly scrubbing.

'Miss Lackland?'

Her head came up, and a delightful smile played across her face. 'Yes. Dr Lackland,' she returned. Her voice was husky, low, almost teasing. 'You must excuse me for a moment,' she chuckled. 'If I don't get this tempera off my hands now I'll be wearing it for a month!' She gestured him to sit down.

Her voice was a soft contralto that sent shivers up Rob's spine. He could not see her clearly. Her figure was feminine, attractive in outline, but it was the mass of hair that startled and held him. The last rays of the sun struck and seemed to be entangled in it, spinning its golden beauty into a halo around her head. She took another step out of the darkness and was suddenly transfigured. She was slightly above five foot six. Entranced as he was with her hair, he could hardly spare a glance for the gamine face with the dimple on each side, the sparkling green eyes, the modest curves hidden in the folds of the white coat.

The impact was more than he could handle, and blood pulsed in his forehead as he struggled to reason things out. He *knew* her—and yet he didn't. All men have dreams about the perfect woman for themselves, and here was his, walking nonchalantly into the room. All his vaunted self-control vanished.

'I've seen you somewhere before,' he blurted. 'I'm sure I have!'

'There's a lot of that going around,' she commented drily as she dropped into the chair opposite him, straightened out her coat to cover her knees, and looked at him primly. 'But unfortunately I've never been there.'

'Where?' There's no end to it, Rob told himself wryly. Once you start acting like a fool, you can hardly stop! Get a grip on yourself, Carlton.

'Wherever it is you think you've seen me,' the woman returned. 'Now, evidently, you've travelled some distance, and you don't have an appointment. Just what can I do for you, Mr——?'

'Carlton,' he furnished, shrugging himself back into his own disguise. 'Robert Carlton, of Carltonworld.'

'How nice for you. And you come from...?'

'New York.' It was coming easier, now that the gloss had taken over, inside and out. 'I came down from New York just to see you.'

She chuckled, that deep-throated contralto again that plucked at his nerves. 'I don't take patients from out of my geographical zone, Mr Carlton. And I'm not a specialist.'

'Damn!' It was meant to be under the breath, but he could not restrain it. She shrugged her shoulders, and a smile chased across her face.

'I wouldn't want to turn you away, though, after all that distance. What seems to be your trouble?'

'I'm not sick,' he said hurriedly. 'I'm not a case of smallpox!'

'That's good to know,' she returned. 'Now I'm sure you have the wrong house. I'm a dentist, Mr Carlton, not a medical doctor.' She moved in her chair, as if to get up, signifying that the interview was over.

'No—lord, no!' he said. 'Wait!'

She looked at him enquiringly and sank back into her chair. He swallowed a couple of times, stood up, and paced a step or two in each direction. Deep breathing. He could feel the power and control returning. His mind spun as he walked. One mark on the good side: Jacob's granddaughter is a professional woman. A dentist? There aren't many female dentists going around these days, but still a professional. A small thing. And, living in this Caribbean backwater, she can't be up on the world's activities. So—just turn on the charm! He flexed the muscles around his mouth, and broke out a smile.

'That's not the way things are, Miss Lackland,' he offered in his best management tone. 'The problem that brought me all this distance has nothing to do with your profession.' *Get in a little personal something, dolt!* 'You have an excellent collection of paintings on your walls. The artist is LaLa?'

She nodded. Her smile had widened to a grin. 'I've seen a number of his works in New York,' Rob continued, getting into his stride. 'You've a small fortune hanging here.'

'I don't think of them in that way,' the woman assured him. 'Your problem is about paintings?'

'No, not at all. You *do* know what Carltonworld is?'

'Of course. We're not *that* far out in the backwoods, Mr Carlton! It's an international conglomerate that makes fifty kinds of dolls and a heap of other garbage. Are you perhaps the reigning Carlton?'

'For my sins,' he laughed. 'I set out to be an electronic engineer, and instead inherited a toy company. And you and I are business partners.'

That caught her up, he thought. A direct shot to the brain, Carlton. She's up straight in her chair, paying some attention!

'You and I are business partners?'

Try the other barrel now, Carlton. Lean on it!

'Your grandfather and my father were partners, Miss Lackland,' Rob explained. 'I understand you to be the only descendant in the Blake line, and I'm the only Carlton. You hold a considerable number of shares in the bank for yourself, so we have a common interest, you and I.'

And that shot missed. What the hell have I said wrong now? She's leaning back in the chair, laughing!

'I'm afraid you've made another mistake,' she gurgled. 'I *am* sorry. You and I have nothing in common, Mr Carlton. You want Emerald.'

'You're not Emerald?'

'No. I'm Laura Lackland. But Emerald is here—someplace.' She seemed to flow out of the chair and glide across the room. 'Belle,' she called, 'see if you can find Emerald and send her in here!'

She studied him as she walked back to her chair and settled into it. A fine figure of a man, that would have been her aunt's description. Big, strong, sleek. Dark eyes, black hair, and more arrogance than any two men ought to have. And I'm not above savouring the classical male, she told herself laughingly. Isn't that what her Aunt Mary was on about during her last visit? 'Why don't you get married, Laura? You're not getting any younger, you know. There aren't as many fish left in the sea as you think. Do you know how quickly the percentage drops as you grow towards thirty?'

Yes, I know, Laura thought. Another couple of years and it will be down to zero. But I'm not all that crazy to get married, am I? I've just started to benefit from my career, I already have a daughter—why would any sane woman want to marry? Look at him. He's puzzling something out, and trying to hide it from me. But I can see the glitter in his eyes. Be careful, Laura. You treat him like a piranha, but he's really a great white shark!

'Laura,' he said slowly. 'Laura Lackland. LaLa?'

'Yes,' she said, and let the word lie there between them.

Rob smacked his temple with one open hand. 'How many kinds of fool have I been so far today?'

And that's a question I wouldn't touch with a ten-foot pole, she smiled to herself. Down, girl! Straight face, honest, sincere expression! It was a struggle, but worth it in the end. And, just as she managed all this, and Rob recovered, a small person bubbled down the hall and limped into the room.

Not a child, and not an adult, eleven-year-old Emerald Lackland, wearing a dripping bathing suit and a big smile. Her two long black braids fell down over her back. Her left leg looked—strange, as if the muscles could not be commanded. Close behind her the other woman came in pursuit, flapping a big towel and a robe in either hand.

'I told her, Miss Laura, but she don't pay me no mind. Dry yourself off, I said, and put on your robe, but she gonna do what she wants, that one.'

'Now, Belle,' soothed Laura. And then, more sharply, 'Emerald!'

'Yes, ma'am!' Like a nervous young filly anxious to be out into the paddock, the girl pawed at the carpet while Belle gave a few swipes with the towel, and offered the robe.

Laura patted the seat next to her. The girl broke into a grin, limped over and plumped herself down. 'This is Mr Carlton, Emerald,' Laura introduced. 'He has some business with you.'

'If you're the truant officer,' the child said in a high clear voice, 'you're making a mistake. I only skipped school one day, and LaLa said—well, she said a great many things, and I was mad at her for days and days—but *then* she said she'd fix it up with the school board. So why did you come?'

The child's command of language was excellent. Her diction was marred only by a sibilant hiss that pursued each word through the interstices of the braces on her front teeth.

'No, no,' Rob hurried to defend himself, 'I'm not anything to do with the school system. Good lord!' He turned back towards Laura with a look of appeal on his face, but all he received was a shrug of the shoulders.

'Emerald,' Laura said, 'you and Mr Carlton are partners in a business, and he has some problems.'

Good lord, he told himself again. The whole damn corporation is in trouble, and it all depends on an eleven-year-old child and a sarcastic dentist! Why me?

# CHAPTER TWO

'I THINK we need considerably more explanation, Mr Carlton,' said Laura, leaning both elbows on the kitchen table, nursing a cup of coffee. Belle had lit the kerosene lamps before she had hustled Emerald off for a bath, and in the soft glow Robert Carlton looked—good enough to eat! Laura smiled to herself. That had been the popular phrase when she was working her way through Tufts University. The shadows seemed to emphasise his facial contours, rather than hide them.

'And what do they call this mountain of yours?' he asked.

She smiled broadly. For the first time, the dimples caught his eye. 'There's only *one* mountain, Mr Carlton, and we call it the Mountain. But we're getting away from the subject, aren't we?'

'I suppose so,' he grinned. Unfair! Laura shouted at herself. Why should one man be *that* lucky! Little bells began ringing in her mind. That smile should be registered as a dangerous weapon; he ought not to be allowed to carry it around in public!

'I suppose so,' he repeated, 'but I can't help being curious about this whole place. What it is, why it is, and why you and Emerald are——'

'And Belle,' she interrupted. 'We couldn't operate without Belle. Why we are here? *My* grandfather owned this house. It was to be his retirement home, but he never got around to that, so he left it to me. And then, when I was about to set up my own practice, the State Department asked me to service the area under a one-year contract, as part of the Peace Corps operations. Finding dentists in these little tropical islands is almost as hard as—dear lord, I was about to use a terrible simile!'

'As pulling hen's teeth?' Rob was perfectly solemn. Laura nodded, smiled back at him, then gave herself a shake to remind herself what sort of man she was dealing with.

'Something like that.' She took another long sip at her coffee; it was one way to keep from falling into those dark, dark eyes of his and drowning. 'Now, about your problem? Why didn't you take it up with our lawyer?'

'You mean you don't know about Mr Ladessy?'

'You mean old Mr Ladessy? Yes, I knew about him. He was a fine friend and adviser. I went up to Connecticut for the funeral. Emerald couldn't go. She was—having trouble at the time. But we still have a lawyer—Mr Frank Ladessy. He lives in California, I believe. I have a letter around here someplace. I—we're so busy, all of us—that I hardly ever get around to reading the mail. You were saying?'

'There's an important stockholders' meeting next month—may I call you Laura?'

'Out of the office, of course,' she returned. 'During business hours I have to be very formal. People around here think I'm rather—young—for my position.'

'I thought you were hardly eighteen, Laura.' Good lord, she thought, how smoothly that comes out! He's had the practice, I suppose. And then, wistfully, I only wish he meant it!

'To be certified in dentistry you need a college undergraduate degree, and then four years of advanced study,' she said. And I'm not about to tell you that I did both in three years apiece, and put in three years in a partnership, and thirty is glaring at me so closely that it frightens me. It's true, what my aunt said—the older a

professional woman gets, the fewer chances there are for
marriage! I can't help but wonder what I'm missing!

Rob coughed to attract her wandering attention. 'Well,
there's a great change to be made in company policies,
Laura, and I need all the votes I can get. So I came down
to ask—well, to ask Emerald if she would sign these
proxies for me.' He reached down for his briefcase, and
had another thought. 'You *are* Emerald's guardian?'

'I'm Emerald's mother,' Laura said firmly. Rob looked
surprised, then turned back to his briefcase and took
out a couple of papers. One of the sample dolls fell out
on to the table.

'All I need is your signature, then, Laura. Laura?'

'I had a Carlton doll when I was very young,' she
sighed, holding the little cuddly form in her hands. 'A
very wonderful doll. It didn't do anything, or say anything—it just lay there and let me love it. Nobody makes
dolls like that any more, do they, Mr Carlton?'

He wasn't about to lie about it; that wasn't his style.
He shrugged his shoulders. 'The world turns,' he said.
'Now, about these proxies——'

'It's late, Mr Carlton——'

'Couldn't you call me Rob?'

'I—is that what your business acquaintances call you?'

'No,' he laughed. 'That's what my mother calls me.'

'Well, in that case, Rob—it's late. This is un-
doubtedly an important item, and Emerald and I owe it
to you to study the proposition carefully. It will take
some time. Meanwhile, I'd suggest you go over to your
hotel and settle in. Tomorrow morning I have office
hours and Emerald has school. In the afternoon I paint,
and I refuse to have those important hours reduced. But
perhaps in the evenings, over five or six days...'

Dear God, Rob thought. Five or six days? There's a
lot to be done back at the office! And Mary was wrong—
the smile doesn't seem to be working on *this* woman.

One more try? 'I'd really planned to return to New York tonight, Laura.' And the *big* smile.

It almost seemed as if she flinched away from the smile. 'Not a chance, Mr Carlton—Rob. Not a chance. At which hotel will you be staying?'

'I haven't any idea,' he returned, his mind turning over at double its normal revolutions. 'Could you suggest something?'

'Dear me!' Laura made a tch-tch sound and shook her head. 'Staying at a hotel in Saba is somewhat of an adventure,' she said. 'All I could recommend is that you try the nearest one, the Windwardside Guest House.'

'Sounds all right to me,' he nodded. 'Perhaps you could telephone ahead for me and make a reservation?'

Another smile as she shook her head slowly, looking down to break contact with those eyes. 'I'd like to, but we don't have a telephone.'

'No electricity? No telephone?' For a moment, pomposity intervened and he made it all sound like a personal insult. His forehead furrowed as he looked down at her. Coupled with the shadows playing across his face, it gave him a satanic look. Laura shuddered, then rose in defence.

'There are both on the island,' she interjected, 'but we're not hooked up to them.'

'Then perhaps you could run me over there in your car?'

She threw up both hands, as a Frenchman might when faced with the ultimate impossibility. 'Also no car,' she said. 'But it's only a mile or two up the mountain, and I *do* have a bicycle. Can you ride?'

Rob shoved his chair back and stood up, laughing inwardly at himself. *How Now, Big Tycoon?* It was hard to keep a straight face. The left corner of his mouth kept twitching.

'I haven't ridden a bike in twenty years,' he admitted ruefully, 'but I understand that once you learn you never forget. Might I leave my jacket and bags?'

'Of course. I'm sorry to inconvenience you.'

'And may I count on the opportunity to convince you to sign those proxies?'

'And Emerald, too,' Laura insisted. 'I'm only her guardian in law—it's still *her* stock.'

'And Emerald, too,' he agreed. She got up from the table and walked by him, and he followed closely behind her, almost treading on her heels. Too close, she told herself. Too big. Too—— God, what am I thinking about?

'Belle and I will take care of your bags,' she promised. 'Don't forget your wallet. The bicycle is out by the shed, and I'll walk you up to the road.'

'I wouldn't want to get lost,' chuckled Rob. It was as old a bicycle as ever he had seen—no gears to shift, no mudguards, either front or rear, and one pedal was broken.

'You don't have to worry about getting lost on Saba,' she teased. 'The island is only five miles square. And as for the road—well, it goes from here to there and no place else. Watch your step. We had the drive smoothed while Emerald required a wheelchair, but now she no longer needs it and the grass is breaking through.'

Watch your step, hell! Rob grinned to himself, following her along and pushing the bicycle. Watch my feet when all that beautiful movement is going on in front of me? Look at how those hips roll! Dr Lackland, you may be your own best medicine! He was so absorbed that when Laura stopped at the edge of the highway he almost ran her down.

'Thataway, Mr Carlton!' She pointed up the incline of the road. 'The only way you can miss it is by running off the edge of the island. Come see us tomorrow—in the evening, for preference. Come to dinner. And— Rob—we're not too formal!'

'I'd love to.' He straddled the bike. The seat was too low for his long legs, but it hardly seemed worthwhile mentioning it. He wobbled badly for the first dozen feet, then seemed to get the hang of it. As he went out of sight around the next zig in the zig-zag road, he heard her warm, deep laughter chasing him on the constant breeze. There was some exhilaration causing his heart to pump faster than usual. Probably it's just from breathing clean air, he told himself, as he put his mind on pumping the old machine.

'Well, you done chased him off?' Belle came up behind Laura as she leaned against the front-door screen. 'Altogether too pretty, that man. Trouble—I see it big. Big trouble!'

'Oh, come on, Belle,' Laura said irritably. 'I thought you gave up your crystal ball years ago. He's probably a nice man. He's a long way from home, and a little confused, and——' Why am I making excuses for him? she thought. Belle's right. 'Is Emerald bathed?' she asked.

'You know she is. Fight or not, I put her in the tub. Lordy, how that child runs on! "But I've been in the pool for hours, Belle. I can't possibly get any cleaner!" Don't have no soap in the pool, I tell her. Can't wash behind the ears when you just swimmin'. C'mon, I got a casserole in the oven, and time we has supper.' Laura smiled and pulled away from the door.

Emerald came in moments later, hair still dripping, draped in her long white granny-gown. Although Saba was a tropical island, Lower Hell's Gate was more than nine hundred feet above sea level, and the winds blew cool at night. 'Did Mr Carlton go, Mama?' asked Emerald.

'Yes, dear, a few minutes ago. He had to find a hotel.'

'And look what he left for me!' The sample doll was
still lying on the table where Laura had dropped it. For
a second she felt a jealous stab. But of course it had to
be Emerald's doll—I'm too old for dolls! she thought.
The child picked up the toy and cuddled it. 'It's soft,
LaLa. And look here—there's a button!'

At the first push, the doll opened and closed its eyes.
Emerald shrieked with excitement, and pushed again.
The doll began to talk—not an extended vocabulary, but
enough to catch their attention. 'I love you. You are a
pretty girl. I'm thirsty.'

'Good heavens!' exclaimed Belle. 'Next thing you
know, they make them human!'

'I suppose so,' Laura sighed. 'You can even make its
hair grow.' She was reading from the little instruction
tag attached to the doll's leg. 'And the whole thing runs
on batteries. I wish I owned a battery factory!'

'Hmph,' snorted Belle. 'You *sell* some of them
paintings, you make enough money to buy a battery
factory. Oh no, LaLa got to *give* them away! Why you
don't sell them?'

'I don't know,' Laura muttered. 'They're all things I
love. You don't sell things you love!'

'An' you don't make peanuts from the dental work!'

'Belle, you know it's a humanitarian project! I'm not
*supposed* to make money.'

'Then you oughta feel good, Miss LaLa, 'cause you
ain't. Food money almost gone for the month. We gonna
live on soup for the last three days.'

'I like soup,' she said defensively. 'Come over here,
sweetheart, while I dry your hair.' The girl came across
the room and stood between Laura's knees while the
towel was applied vigorously, followed by an equally
vigorous brushing. Belle glowered at the pair of them,
puttered around the little gas stove, and slammed a few
dishes down on the table.

'An' you knows better to brush all that hair at my table while we gettin' supper,' she grumbled. 'Hair over everything. I taught you better than that!'

'I know you did, Belle. I'm sorry.'

'Just because you a doctor now, it don't mean you can forget all your upbringing!'

'I *said* I was sorry, Belle. And I could hardly forget that you brought me up. I wouldn't want to.' No, I wouldn't want to. The picture flashed back. Laura Lackland, too small to see over the top of the bed where her mother lay dying, clutching desperately at her older sister Anne's fingers while strange words rumbled from the throat of the big man who was her grandfather. Trying not to cry, because Grandfather said people don't do that—until Belle came up behind her and swept her out of the room and into the warmth and comfort of the kitchen, where she could cry to her heart's content. Dear Belle, who was a half-mother to Laura. And dear Anne, twelve years older, who had been the other half.

'Oh now, Miss Laura, I didn't mean for to make you cry,' said Belle quickly.

'I'm not crying, Belle—don't be silly. I've just got—something in my eye. Stand still, Emerald. I'll never get these braids right if you keep wriggling!'

The atmosphere lightened as the simple meal was served. Emerald, not easily put down, chattered about her day at school. 'And I don't need the pain pills to-night, LaLa. It didn't hurt at all today.'

'Well, isn't that wonderful!' Laura told her, adding a hug for dessert. 'Dr Friedland said it would get all better this time, didn't he?'

'He sure did. He's a wonderful man. But it's been a long time, and I hate that exercise machine.'

'We'll be going over to see him fairly soon,' Laura promised, smoothing the soft black hair. 'You've been very brave, sweetheart. And by this time *next* year you'll be running around with all the other kids, having a wild time.'

'I am very good and brave, aren't I?' The emerald-green eyes stared up at Laura innocently.

'Yes——' A very doubtful response from one who had learned the hard way how tricky raising children can be.

'Then I can play my records tonight, LaLa, and listen to the radio, and——'

'And first we'll do the homework!'

'Aw—but, Mama!'

'Aw—but, Emerald! Homework first, fun later. In the living-room at my desk. Get started while I do the dishes.'

The child went, reluctantly, but in a few minutes they could hear her singing. 'You lucky,' Belle told Laura. '*You* was the meanest kid in the world. Emerald, she don't stay mad long enough to make no trouble!'

Laura smiled, fingering the doll that the little girl had left by her chair. 'You're telling me that I was a difficult child to raise?'

'Difficult? Impossible! Harum-scarum. You wouldn't believe you wasn't a boy. Never thought you'd grow up to be a lady, that's what!'

Laura chuckled as she moved around to clear the table. 'I'll do that,' said Belle.

'No, we had that argument before. Whoever cooks the meal doesn't do the clearing up. You go sit a while with Emerald, and read the paper. There isn't much to do here.'

Belle smiled at her, and ambled out of the kitchen. And you're not getting any younger, Miss Belle, Laura thought. Sooner, rather than later, we have to make life easier for you. Maybe I'd *better* sell some pictures. Or insist that the government pay at least my *last* year's salary. Or stop spending so much of it on dental supplies and paints! Laughing, Laura struggled into her washing-up gloves, and was hard at it until a noise outside the house interrupted.

It sounded like an old tank in a war movie. On Saba, where nights were so still one could hear the wind whispering through the trees, and the peeping of tree frogs, *any* noise was unusual.

'Miss Laura, come quick!' Belle, agitated, and behind Belle's voice, the giggling laughter of Emerald. So it wasn't exactly an emergency, Laura decided. Just a minor crisis? She stripped off her rubber gloves and left the sink to its dishes.

Both Belle and Emerald were standing out on the small concrete stoop outside the door. Emerald was dancing up and down with glee. Belle looked astonished, standing there with her hands upraised, leaning against the half-opened screen door.

'Well, shut the door at least,' complained Laura, 'or we'll have a house full of crawlers and flyers.' Belle moved aside so she could come out. It was long past sunset, but there was moon enough to see. A battered old jeep steamed and complained past to the house. It might once have been olive drab, now it was painted brilliant red, with a high luminescent yellow canvas roof spread over the top on light aluminium rods. And, struggling to get out of the driver's seat, Mr Carlton.

'You've got Mr Sundlip's taxi!' Emerald yelled gleefully.

'He ever knows you steal his vehicle, he gonna kill you dead,' Belle declared solemnly.

'We didn't expect you back so soon, Mr Carlton.' Laura tried to sound cool and detached, but found it hard to do so. For some reason his return both excited and irritated her.

'I discovered a small problem.' He grinned at her as he lifted her bicycle out of the back seat. 'And not a dent on it,' he continued, rolling it over to Laura. 'And it's *not* true!'

'What's not true?' Somehow I've come into a three-reel movie, she told herself, and I don't know what the plot is, or which one is the villain!

'That old saying that once you've learned to cycle you never forget! I fell off three times before I got to the village, and once more right in front of the hotel.'

'Why, you poor man,' soothed Belle. 'Come in the house this minute, and let me doctor you.'

'He doesn't seem to be bleeding, Belle,' Laura snapped.

'And I didn't steal the car either,' he chuckled. 'No, I stopped at the hotel long enough to wash off my wounds and to—seek a little Dutch courage. I tried to rent the vehicle, but the owner would have no part of that, so I bought it from him.'

'You bought it from him?' Emerald stood aghast. 'Autos cost a bundle on the island! You must be——'

'Emerald! Ladies don't ask gentlemen that sort of thing!' The child took one look at Laura's grim expression, but was not ready to give up the ship.

'They do if they want to marry them,' she stated simply.

'That's enough, young lady. March yourself into the house and finish your homework. Now!'

The child hesitated, then walked back into the house. 'Besides, I'm only a kid, not a lady,' she muttered as she went past her mother. The remark earned her a pat on her posterior. Both mother and daughter were laughing after the exchange. Laura turned around to Rob.

'I suppose you came for your luggage?'

'Not exactly.' There was the smallest twist of a smile at the corners of his mouth. 'I have this problem.'

'Oh?' I have an idea that I won't want to hear about this problem, Laura thought fiercely, but her manners interfered with her good sense. 'What is it?' she asked.

'It seems I'm here in the middle of the tourist season,' Rob continued. 'The Windwardside Guest House is full up—all four rooms are occupied. So the manager called the Captain's Quarters. They have one of their ten rooms empty, but the roof leaks, and they don't expect to get it repaired very soon.'

'Don't tell me,' she sighed. 'And the Bottom Guest House and the Caribe Guest House are all full, too?'

'All nine rooms between them.' Rob shook his head dolefully. 'However, the manager at Windwardside *did* say that, in emergency cases like this, there was someone who would occasionally put up a visitor. A Dr Lackland, in Lower Hell's Gate?'

Laura sighed and shook her head gently. Her hands were folded together at her breast as she thought—though perhaps *thought* was too strong a word for a mind that was running in circles. Come into my parlour, said the spider to the fly? Trouble, wasn't that what Belle said. *Big* trouble. But the night was moving gently on, and things would get no better for waiting. And besides, she could charge him a bundle, and perhaps refurbish the food budget?

'Yes, I do,' she said slowly, amazed at how hard it was to keep her voice level. 'But you realise that, with all the disruptions to our household, I would have to charge you a very high price?'

Rob was grinning again. Damn the man! 'How much?' he asked.

'Sixteen dollars a night, American!' Laura said it all in a rush, hoping he would find it too dear, and then hoping that he would not. 'That includes three meals a day, of course.'

'Of course.' The grin had disappeared. He was thinking things over, she told herself. *So I know the price is too high; I've only ever charged eight dollars before this!* Rob pursed his lips a couple of times, and nodded.

'Done,' he said.

'Well, I——' she stuttered. 'I——'

'Come you in,' invited Belle from behind Laura's shoulder. 'No use to stand out in the moon where the *obeah* man can get you.'

'There aren't any *obeah* men on Saba,' snapped Laura.

'Haiti!' Rob Carlton exclaimed. 'I knew I could place it! Haiti—right, Miss Belle?'

'Many years gone, when I was a little girl,' Belle told him. The pair of them went into the house and down to the kitchen, leaving Laura standing outside by herself, wondering.

She walked over and patted the hood of the jeep. 'His faithful steed, I suppose,' she murmured. 'And on his side, without a doubt!' The jeep gave a tired grunt and seemed to settle a little closer to the earth. 'Coward!' she laughed, and went into the house.

'Mama?'

'Yes, dear?'

'I'm stuck on this arithmetic problem.'

'Just a minute, dear.'

Laura strode down the hall to the kitchen. Rob was sitting at the table, being plied with coffee by a very solicitous Belle. 'An', you know, he don't even stop for dinner. The poor man must be starved!'

'Haven't eaten a thing since that plastic meal on the plane,' he commented.

'Well, I jus' happen to have a piece of steak in the refrigerator,' Belle said happily. 'I fix you, man. Steak, french fries. Beer? No, we don't have no beer. Water is nice—rainwater. Best in the Indies, no?'

'I wouldn't mind,' he returned. 'Although I'd love a cup of coffee—caffeine is my favourite addiction. Will you join me, Miss Laura?'

Across the table, half in shadow, Belle was shaking her head negatively. 'No, thank you,' said Laura as she skirted the table and went back to the dishes in the sink. 'We get casserole and he gets steak?' she hissed under her breath.

'He a man. Man gotta have steak,' Belle whispered. 'Don't ask for no coffee—only got one cup left. Tomorrow breakfast you gotta have cocoa!'

Laura made a few washing noises with the dishes, but her heart wasn't in it. She dried her hands. 'I forgot— Emerald needs some help with her homework,' she said. 'Excuse me.'

They both beamed at her. Like I was the idiot daughter of some poor neighbour! she snarled at herself as she left the room. She stopped in the hall and took a couple of deep breaths. Nobody can make you feel inferior if you don't help them! she told herself sternly. One of Grandfather's favourite phrases. She straightened her shoulders and walked slowly into the living-room.

'What's the problem?' she asked.

'Oh, I got it figured out, Mama. Now I just have to do this history report. Did you know that Columbus sighted Saba in September 1493, but he couldn't come ashore because there was no place to land?'

'No, I didn't know that.' Laura picked up the latest copy of her trade magazine and leafed through the pages. From the kitchen came the smell of cooked steak. I wonder if he likes it rare? she asked herself hungrily. The casserole had tasted fine as it went down, but it had been a month or more since she had sunk her teeth into a nice rare steak. *And a husband and wife ought to know each other's tastes.* She stopped to think about *that* wild interruption. Husband and wife? Good God, my aunt's lectures are catching up to me! she thought.

'And did you know that Saba has changed hands from Dutch to English to Spanish to French twelve times since then?'

'Well, I knew it was a lot,' she returned. 'But now it's Dutch, dear.'

'You bet,' laughed Emerald. 'Which is why English is the major language on the island, and we use American money. I wonder if Queen Beatrix really knows we exist?'

'Of course she—well, perhaps not about you and me,' Laura said cautiously. The only thing she *was* sure of was that inaccurate answers at home generally arrived in the school the next day, much out of context.

'Mr Carlton is a nice man, Mama. I wonder if he's married?'

'I—I really don't know, Emerald. Finish your homework.'

'It is—I finished every bit of it. Is he going to stay here with us?'

'For a day or two, I suppose. He wants to talk to both of us about a business matter. And then I'm sure he'll want to go back to New York.'

'Whatever for? I read that they have the biggest crowds and the dirtiest air in America. Who would want to live there?'

'I—don't have any answer, love. I lived in a big city once, when I was going to dental school. In Boston. It had lots of things Saba doesn't. Television, movies, plays, opera, symphonies.' And I never could take time off to see any of them. Dear lord, what a stick-in-the-mud I've been! And what a prude the men in all my classes must have thought me to be! 'We can't stay on Saba for ever, darling. My contract is up shortly, and it's time we started planning on where we would really like to go. And speaking of going, right now you're going to bed, Miss Muffet. School day tomorrow.'

'But I want to talk to Mr Carlton!' protested Emerald.

'Tomorrow, dear. Or some day.'

'How about right now?' Rob came into the room, a satisfied smile on his face. 'I'm a proud uncle, owned by three nieces and one nephew, and loaded with bedtime stories. Why don't I put the young lady to bed, and you can finish your dishes in peace, Laura?'

I'd like to finish my dishes in pieces, right on the top of your head, she told herself. But the two of them, Emerald and Rob Carlton, seemed to have made an instant attachment to each other, and it took energy to refuse. 'All right. Come along.'

She started off down the hall at Emerald's pace, then stopped and looked back. The big New York tycoon was swinging her daughter up on his back, giving her a piggyback to bed. And how can a poor dentist compete with *that*? she asked herself as she opened the door to Emerald's room and turned down the covers.

There was a great deal of giggling and wriggling as the story started. *Little Red Riding Hood*. And what could go wrong with that? Laura asked herself as she wandered away towards the dishes. Her feet were disinclined to move away from the door of the bedroom. She had to compel them. No doubt about it, Rob was a great storyteller.

The only thing that saved her sanity that evening was that Belle had finished the dishes before she got back to the kitchen.

# CHAPTER THREE

THE NOISE woke Rob up at five-thirty—susurrus of whisperings and small movements, and an occasional grunt. He managed to get to the window and look out. A line of people in single file stood or sat next to the house, extending from around the corner behind him out to the driveway. Men, women, children—but mostly children. They maintained their places in the slow-moving line patiently, even pleasantly. About half of them carried little bouquets of flowers. Go back to sleep, he told himself. He dropped back into the warmth of the huddled blankets, but found no peace. 'Might as well get breakfast,' he muttered, as he fumbled for clean underwear and trousers.

He was still grumbling to himself as he discovered the bathroom and made himself ready to face the day. One of the closed doors in the hall intrigued him. It bore a big cardboard sign with the word 'NO' printed in red on one side, and 'YES' on the other. The 'NO' side was turned outward. He would have investigated, but the clatter of dishes reminded him how hungry he was. He made his way down the hall and turned towards the kitchen. Belle was busy inside, and must have sensed his presence.

'Good morning, Mr Carlton. You an early riser. Miss Laura say you surely not be up before nine. Hungry?'

'I could eat a horse,' he chuckled. 'But coffee first?'

Belle's face fell. 'We don't have no coffee, Mr Carlton. I think to go to the grocery before you are up, but——'

'I drank all your coffee last night?'

'Surely you did. Poor Miss Laura, she only got one eye open for surgery this morning.'

'Oh, is that what's going on?'

'Well, is unusual, you know, to be the only dentist on the island. People come from all over. Some don't even have troubles, but Miss Laura, she do something for them all.'

'How far to the store, Belle?' asked Rob.

'Not far—ten minutes' walk, maybe. I don't have horse for breakfast. You want eggs, ham, bacon?'

'All of the above,' he laughed. 'But first, why don't you and I climb in my car and go to the store for coffee?'

She gave him a big smile, then it fell in on her. 'Can't do that,' she sighed. 'I run out of house money.'

'You can't be serious, Belle!'

'Serious, all right. Very serious. Miss Laura, she all the time spend money on things not covered in contract, you know, and don't charge nothin' for her work, not even for her paintings!'

'Good lord! Those paintings are worth a fortune!' he exclaimed.

'Hey, what I tell you, Emerald?' The little girl was just coming in through the back door, soaking wet, shivering in her one-piece swimsuit. 'You hear? You mama's paintings worth lots of money. How the exercise go this morning?'

'Pretty good, Belle. Can I have some breakfast?' The child swathed herself in a fluffy towel and sat down at the table. 'Mr Carlton.' A greeting, cheerful enough, but not enthusiastic. 'I hate to do it in the morning. Six times up and down the pool, three times a day. But very soon now——'

'Very soon you'll be a championship swimmer,' Rob interjected. Emerald smiled at that, smiled with her heart.

'Do you really think so? I go to see the doctor in another few days—for the last time. And then I'm going to be able to run and jump—and maybe be a championship swimmer. But not today.' Rob looked over the child's head at Belle. Her eyes cautioned him to get off the subject.

'Come on, Belle,' he urged. 'While Emerald is eating you and I can zoom up to the store and be back before anyone knows it.'

'But——'

'But everything will be taken care of.'

'Ah. Very well, we go. Emerald, eat the breakfast food. And remember, if we be late, the school bus comes at eight o'clock.'

'I like to ride in cars too,' the little girl complained mournfully.

'And you will,' promised Rob, 'but not today. Belle?'

They were the only gasoline-powered vehicle on the road.

'Everybody seems to be going someplace!' shouted Rob, as they turned on to the main highway.

'The only time,' Belle returned. 'It don't get hot like in Sint Maarten, but we like to work the day until noon. Turn right here.'

The market was a combination of open-air vegetable stands, and a few stores stocked mainly with canned foods. 'Get everything we need,' ordered Rob, then stood back in amazement as Belle skimmed through the area, ordering with lightning speed, with the separate packages being delivered directly to the jeep by the entrepreneurs. Their last stop was at the separate market for meat and milk. 'Goat's milk,' Belle told him. 'You will learn to love it.'

'And if I don't?'

'Then you gonna be without milk until you go back to New York,' she laughed. 'OK, we go now. I got plenty coffee.'

Rob drove more slowly on the way back. There was something he had to know. 'What happened to Emerald's leg?' he asked.

'Ah, that. She was—what you call—birth defect. Six operations she's had. This was the last one, we hope. Poor child has life full of woe. Miss Laura, she rescue that kid, believe me.'

'And Miss Laura is her mother?'

'You better believe, man. Her father too, for that matter.'

'And Miss Laura—what about *her* mother?'

'Ah, her! I am only new come to United States then. When Miss Laura is three years old her mother dies. For a while, her sister Anne is her mother. Miss Laura think her sister a saint. Well, she is not that, maybe, but very good woman, you understand? Much older than LaLa. And then, when there is the accident, then I take Miss Laura to her grandpa, and Emerald, too.' Rob wanted to ask for more, so badly that he could taste it, but they had arrived at the house.

Emerald skipped out to meet them. 'Ooh, what a lot of things you bought, Belle, and it's not even the first of the month! The bus is coming!' She limped up to the jeep, gave Belle a kiss, and disappeared up the path, making good speed despite her handicap.

'It doesn't seem to bother her, does it?' Rob remarked, watching the girl hurry up the hill.

'Bother her? Miss Laura don't *let* it bother her. She talk to her all the time, and cheer her up, and make her think *other* kids got it bad 'cause *they* don't have their own doctor to worry over them! Some pair, those two. They got what Miss Laura call "mutual admiration society!" Too bad these groceries ain't gonna walk into the kitchen by themselves.'

Rob turned around and grinned down at her, and Belle grinned back. The gold tooth right in the middle of her

mouth splashed reflected sunlight in his eyes. He went
up on his toes and stretched every muscle in his body.
As he loaded up his arms with bags and containers, the
life of a work-harried tycoon seemed very far away
indeed.

'I thought we didn't have any more coffee, Belle.' Laura
was perched on a high stool between two dental chairs
when Rob slid the mug up to her elbow from behind. A
patient sat in each chair. When she had finished work
on the one side she turned to the other, while an assistant took the first patient away and brought in another. On the far side of the room another girl smiled
at him as she rode the stationary bicycle that provided
electricity for the dental equipment.

He waited until both Laura's hands were out of the
patient's mouth. 'We got some more,' he said. Her hand
jumped and she whirled around, red-faced. Even startled,
she looks a wonder, he told himself. More than twenty
today, but not much more, with her hair fastened in a
no-nonsense bun behind her neck, her white smock immaculate, and those two dimples beaming at him. 'I
thought I'd come and see what goes on in the dentist's
office,' he told her. 'Can I help?'

'I don't think so,' she offered, sipping at the coffee
and going back to work. 'What I'm doing is a form of
*triage*—sorting out those with little problems that can
be fixed immediately, and scheduling appointments for
those with worse difficulties. In addition, I give every
child a fluoride treatment.'

'Bad teeth in Paradise?'

'There are bad teeth or crooked teeth everywhere,
Mr—er—Rob. Years ago, Saba made its living on sugar
cane. The business is dead, but the cane is still everywhere. The children chew it the way American kids chew
gum. So what I try to do is dental prevention more than

dental cure. If I can get the children well, oh dear—look at this poor kid's overbite!'

Rob peered over her shoulder, feeling somewhat lost in a world defined by a strange language. 'Overbite?'

'His upper teeth don't line up with his lowers. It makes it difficult for him to chew.'

'And you can do something about that?'

'While they're young, yes.'

'One more, doctor,' said the young assistant. 'And she's frightened half to death and screaming.'

'That's what you can do for me,' Laura told him, not looking up from her present patient. 'Go and try out that smile of yours on the child. Please?'

Rob grinned down at the back of her head. Please? Smile? This sweet little thing is trying to tell me something that has nothing to do with teeth. She's on to the famous Carlton smile, I do believe! So I'll try it out on the patient. I didn't come all this way to—or maybe I did! He chuckled as he went out into the garden.

The whole business area was almost completely cut off from the house itself. It stood in a separate cement-block building, with a domed glass roof, the whole surrounded by wandering paths through flowerbeds, and cut off from the swimming pool by a tall hedge. For the first time, too, he noticed that a segment of the back of the house had that same sort of roof, a dome of glass facing westward. The little patient was sitting on a child-size bench in the middle of the garden. Her mother was having little effect, and the tears matched the sobs. Rob walked over and crouched down in front of them. And smiled.

The child managed a few more sobs, then, caught by the new attraction, rubbed her eyes with her knuckles and stared. And what do I do now? he asked himself. Just smile? Apparently, it was the right solution. The child managed to clear her eyes, stared at him for a moment, then offered a reluctant little grin of her own.

'I'm the doctor's assistant,' he said softly. 'I'm vice-president in charge of smiling. You have a *lovely* smile.'

The girl shifted in her mother's lap and straightened up. Her little grin became a big smile. He matched it, then laughed. The patient followed suit. There they were, both laughing at each other, when the dental assistant came out. Rob held up a hand signalling for her to wait a minute.

'The doctor is a special friend of mine,' he coaxed. 'A wonderful lady who makes smiles even lovelier. What's your name?'

'Elisa. But it hurts, doesn't it?'

'Not with Dr Lackland. Her name is Laura, did you know that?'

'Is that what you call her?'

'Why, of course. But not in her office, you see.'

'Is she your girlfriend?'

'Why—yes, I believe so.' He stood up, laughing. Caught in your own trap, Carlton! Out of the mouths of babes! He extended a hand. Elisa found the hand and managed to grab two fingers, and they walked together into the office, and introduced themselves.

'Well, Mr Carlton, you proved to be better than Novocaine.' Laura was sitting at the kitchen table, savouring her cup of coffee. Instant coffee. Rob was at the stove, heating more water.

'All in a day's work,' he returned, joining her at table with his own mug. 'And you go through this every day?'

'Oh lord, no. On Monday, Wednesday, and Friday.'

'Aha! Like all medical people, you play golf on Tuesday?'

She gave him a solemn look. As if she were saying down, boy! he thought. She looks tired. It's almost noon, and lord knows how long she's been at it. Since sunrise? For one mad instant he felt like leaning across the table and pulling the pins from that stupid bun. Laura might have read his thoughts, for she did the pulling herself, and shook her head. The beautiful golden curls fell down in mad disarray around her shoulders, and Rob caught his breath, as he had in that first moment of introduction. He had to shake his head to bring himself out of his dream.

'So what *do* you do on the other days?' he persisted.

'Tuesday, Thursday and Saturday, I see the patients who needed appointments for more work. Sunday, I rest.'

'I see. Six days a week from six in the morning until noon?'

'Sometimes until one o'clock,' she corrected. 'But never beyond that. The afternoons I keep for my own private projects.'

'Painting?'

Her head came up from her coffee mug, and he could feel the weight of those cool green eyes studying him. Many a woman had assessed him for their own purposes over the years, but not like this. He could almost see Laura weighing his very soul in the balance; it was a formidable feeling. What if I don't pass the test? he thought. Without even thinking about it logically, he knew he would be missing something important in his life.

'You don't have the priorities right, Mr Carlton,' she said. 'I have projects—plural. My daughter comes first, in both importance and priority. And then after that I paint, if time allows. A little girl only grows up once, and it's extremely important for me to be with Emerald when she wants me—or needs me.'

'I can understand that.' Rob was fumbling with his words and thoughts. 'I've spent most of my adult life managing things. But I can understand what you mean.'

'Can you really, Mr Carlton? I wonder?' Laura looked up at him and offered a small smile, pleasant but limited. 'Have another cup of coffee, Mr—er—Rob. You remember my saying I had a Carlton doll when I was young? I carried it everywhere with me. It didn't say anything, or do anything, it just absorbed love. In fact, if you'll take a peep in Emerald's room, you'll find the same doll, tucked in her bed, I suspect. She loves dolls, too.'

He smiled at her, setting his mug down on the table. The chairs were a little lightweight for a man his size and weight. Laura watched as he arranged things to his satisfaction. 'I know what you're getting at,' he said, 'but, in this modern world, to build a doll or a car or a house that lasts for ever, that's bad business. We build for obsolescence, Laura. We need customers who'll buy every year.'

'Is that the way of it?' she asked softly. 'Then there are lots of little girls who grow up and have nothing to remind them how happy they were. It's not a crime, Rob, but it *is* a disappointment. Well, if you'll excuse me, I must have my noontime swim, and then I'll get to work.'

'How about Emerald?'

'She's in school. It closes at about three o'clock, and the bus takes about fifteen minutes to get her back home.'

'You don't mind if I talk to her?' he asked.

'Of course not. Feel free. You're part of her education.'

'Now you're really making me feel like an institution! I—— '

'Miss Laura, how come you not in the pool?' Belle came bustling out to them. 'You fifteen minutes late already.'

'I know, Belle—I was just going. Did you bring a bathing suit, Rob?'

'No. I hardly expected to go swimming in Chicago.'

'If you'll excuse me, then——'

Laura went off, whistling. It struck Rob that he hardly ever heard a girl whistling these days. There was an aura of happiness about her. The swinging stride as she walked, the bouncing hair, the dimpled smile—he watched her out of sight.

'That some lady.' Belle almost spoke his thoughts. 'Only she not gettin' any younger, man.'

'Younger for what?' he asked

'What you think, man? Younger for gettin' married. That girl a fine dentist. Look, she fix my tooth for me, long time ago when she is still a student. And it one fine tooth.' The big smile came, and the gold tooth in the middle sparkled. 'Wanted to make it nice and white to match, she did. But me, I know. Gold makes the best tooth in the mouth, huh?'

'It seems to,' Rob acknowledged warily. 'She wants to get married?'

'Course she don't wanna get married—not her! But me, *I* want her to get married. Mr Carlton, I raise that girl from a puppy—me and her sister Anne. Best thing for a woman, to have her own man and her own children! Best thing in the world. But Miss Laura, she too stubborn, too choosy. No, she don't wanna get married. But just the same—you married, man?'

'Why, no, but she has her daughter Emerald.'

'Sure,' muttered Belle, 'but she ain't married, you know?'

'I don't quite follow,' returned Rob. 'Her sister Anne was Emerald's mother?'

'No, of course not,' Belle said scornfully.

'And Anne? She was married?'

'Surely she was. She married that Jonathan Blake. A nice man.'

'Then Jonathan Blake was Emerald's father?'

'No, sir. Of course not!'

And now you've got me completely confused, Rob thought to himself. Emerald has inherited Jacob Blake's fortune, but she's *not* his grandchild? Sister Anne is not the mother. Jonathan Blake is *not* the father. The kid's name is Lackland, and Laura claims *she* is the child's mother! I've got to find a telephone, fast!

'Is there an overseas telephone or cable office on the island, Belle?' he asked.

'I 'spect so. I don't know exactly where. Down in Bottom, I suppose.'

'Down where?'

'Bottom, Mr Carlton.' Laura came back down the hall, dressed in a bikini that did much for style and nothing for modesty. Not only was it brief, but it was also beige, so close to matching her skin colour that for a moment he thought her naked. He took a long look. Until that moment he had paid attention only to her hair and her face. Now the hair was under a white bathing cap, and his eye could wander. Square shoulders; tiny but square. Smooth, tanned skin. Small, pert breasts that obviously did not depend on the swimsuit for support. A narrow waist which his hands might span. Swelling hips, well curved. Shapely legs that seemed to go on for ever.

'Wh-what?' he stammered.

'Bottom is the name of our capital city.' Laura wasn't too sure about the expression on his face. If he were not so obviously a man of the world she would have called it stupefaction. 'It's the biggest city on Saba, located within the crater.'

'Ah, so that's where the name comes from?'

'Not exactly. The name comes from the Dutch—*botte*, meaning bowl. It sits inside the crater—inside the bowl.

The telephone and telegraph office is in the centre of the city. Are you planning a trip to the city?'

'Yes, I am. Almost instantly.'

'Would you do us a favour?'

'Why, of course. Anything.'

Laura went over to Belle and the two women had a conference, so low-voiced that Rob could not overhear. Or rather an argument, for there was a difference of opinion, and finally an agreement. 'I hate to impose on you, Mr Carlton, but I wonder if you could take Belle with you to the bank? We're running short of money at the moment, and ——'

'I'd be happy to loan you some money, Laura,' he told her. 'More than happy.'

She waved his offer away. 'There's no need. We have money in the bank, but not here. And I've decided to sell one or two paintings. Belle will mail a letter of instruction to my agent in New York. It wouldn't be convenient?'

'Oh, it would be very convenient,' he assured her. 'I'll need a guide.'

'I doubt it,' Laura laughed. 'Not on this island.'

Ah, but I do, Rob told himself while he nodded agreement. I need a guide through the maze of the Blake family. And the only one around here who wants to talk is obviously Belle!

'Then I take five—ten minutes to get ready,' Belle announced, 'and we go. What you think, Mr Carlton? Bottom is only three miles away, and I don't go there for three months!'

The two women walked out, Laura out of the back door to the pool, and Belle up the hall towards her room. Now what's that all about? Rob asked himself. I suppose I ought to get my notes and things together, and—— But whatever his good intentions he was glued to the back door, watching.

Laura walked to the far end of the pool, positioned herself on the low diving-board, and stretched to the sky. At this distance her bikini looked even more like her skin. He saw her as an arched nude nymph, hands stretched up towards the sun. She bounced a couple of times to get the feel of the board, then effortlessly floated in the air and disappeared under the water, leaving hardly a splash behind to mark her passage.

Rob watched carefully for her reappearance. There was a slight disturbance at the near end of the pool, then nothing. A foot appeared briefly again at the far end of the pool. He was about to run to the rescue when Laura surfaced in the middle, floated gently on to her back, and paddled with a gentle backstroke over to the ladder, having completed two and a half lengths of the pool underwater.

'All ready,' Belle announced from behind him, and he took a deep breath. He was an Olympic-class swimmer himself, but not in the same league with this mermaid, Carlton! he reminded himself.

'Isn't there anything this woman can't do?' he murmured. Belle came over beside him and smiled.

'Plenty,' she sighed. 'That poor girl, she don't know to laugh, and she don't know to cry. Always bundled up in herself, Miss Laura. How you say it—controlled? What she need is to throw dishes, crash on the floor, or jump up and down and scream, or find some man who kiss her to jelly, that one. You ready?'

The old jeep responded magnificently as they followed the road up the incline and on to the plateau where Windwardside village was sited. Larger than Hell's Gate, Windwardside was still a quaint collection of white plaster houses and red-tiled roofs separated by narrow lanes that could hardly contain a car. Women were everywhere, but few men. The highway swung around the city and out to the edge of the plateau, where for two breathtaking miles it clung to the edge of precipitous cliffs a thousand feet above the swells of the Caribbean Sea. The mountain went up as sharply on their right as it went down on their left. The road seemed almost like a bridge over infinity. Above them, the brown barren crags loomed. Higher, they could see the fringes of vegetation, where tropical life, plentifully watered, ran rampant.

It was hard to drive and talk at the same time, but it was information Rob wanted, and he wanted it badly.

'You say that Laura's sister was in an accident, Belle?'

'Bad,' she replied. 'Her and Jonathan both, with the baby. Them two they got killed dead, but the baby, she don't get killed. So Miss Laura, she come out of that hospital and she take the baby and bring her home to us, and from that time she don't smile, she don't laugh. She is only a young thing herself, then, but from that day she grow hundred years old, no?'

'Ah, I see. That must have been difficult. Then the baby was Anne's?'

'No, man—poor Anne, she can't have no baby. The baby belongs to Laura, but she is just starting school, you know, so she give Emerald to Anne, and they have the accident. A long time ago. Lucky. Emerald don't remember them things. She only a baby, not even one years old. Hey, keep you eye on the road, man! We fall off *this* road, they ain't even gonna find pieces!'

For the next few minutes, Rob concentrated on the road, which finally delivered them out of the edge of space and on to another plateau, and a crossroads. He pulled to a stop at the signs.

'Straight ahead,' prodded Belle. 'Turn left and you go down to Fort Bay. Nothing down there but Customs House.'

'I understand, Belle. I'm just trying to catch my breath.'

'Ah,' she laughed. 'That road make Christians out of all drivers on this island. I never think you——'

'Never think I what?'

The black hand came over and patted his wrist gently. 'Take all the time,' she responded. 'Miss Laura say you a tycoon. I figure that be something like a marine? A marine would never be scared to ride on cliffs, no?'

'Probably not,' Rob chuckled. 'But no, I was never a marine. Tell me, Belle, did you know old Mr Blake?'

'Mr Jacob? Sure. He come half a dozen times to see Emerald. Loved that baby, he did. But I think—when they bury his son, Jacob is not the man he used to be, you know? I think it finally kill him. We gonna go now? Bank got bank hours, close at two o'clock!'

'OK, we'll go now.' The jeep sounded as if it resented the order, but it puttered along as they wound their way over the farm-covered plains towards the city.

'Saba grows everything,' Belle pointed out. 'All kinds vegetables, where there was only sugarcane. Nobody grows cane any more. Food only. To import is expensive.'

They came to the lip of the crater. Rob took one look down the road, shifted into third gear, and started off. The breeze stopped as soon as they went over the edge, and the temperature began to climb. He could feel the sweat accumulating on his forehead. By the time they reached the bottom of the bowl and started into the city he could tell they were in the heart of the tropics.

Bottom was like Windwardside, only bigger—red roofs, stone churches, narrow streets, and a clinging heat. 'I get off next corner,' Belle directed. 'You go one more block to telephone building, then I walk down to meet you, no?'

'Yes,' he responded absent-mindedly. He stopped the jeep at the kerb and watched the little old lady bustle, not bothered by the heat at all. 'Time to think,' he told the jeep. It rattled a weak fender at him and said nothing.

Think, big-shot. The baby is Laura's. She gave the child to Anne, and reclaimed it when her sister died. But Laura has never been married. And Jacob Blake had seen the child? And evidently thought she was his grand-daughter. But how could she be if Laura is her mother? What do we have here, a whole flim-flam scheme to get control of Jacob's money?

But if *any* of that is true, what we're saying is that Laura is an unmarried mother with an illegitimate daughter, running a scheme to deprive *somebody* of a whole lot of bucks. And that picture doesn't agree in any way with the sweet, dependable, secure little dentist that I've just met. Does it?

And to take it a little further, he mused, if what I've concluded is true, then neither Laura Lackland nor her daughter Emerald have any claim to vote on the issues coming up in Carltonworld. Her votes would be invalid by reason of fraud—and my idiot brother-in-law might very well wind up running *my* corporation into the ground. That's the only direction he knows to run a business!

He sat in the vehicle for another five minutes, thinking about the dilemma. It all revolved around Laura. Sweet, cunning, unscrupulous Laura. Excitement built up in him. It was impossible to overlook the effect she had on him. Not just sexual; he had seen a thousand women more beautiful, more sexy. But there was that some-thing—that appeal that drew him towards her. An appeal that he wanted to surrender to; or did he? There was no real room in his life for someone like Laura, and this excitement building up inside him was like the call of the hunter to the quarry.

A little smile tickled the corners of his lips, the sort of smile his business enemies took for a warning. He

started the jeep and went down the street to the next
block. Parking space was no problem. There were vehicles in the streets, but most of them horse-drawn. He
stopped in a couple of stores and made some purchases
before he went on.

The post office was one small, cramped room in
Government House. When Rob came in, everyone
stopped to look at him.

'Am I wearing my clothes backwards?' he asked the
young woman at the counter. She giggled and ducked
her head before answering.

'No, sir,' she said in impeccable English. 'You look
exactly right. It's just that—well, the population of Saba
is nine hundred and seventy-nine people, and you are
not one of them. A stranger is always of interest. How
may I help you?'

'I would like to make a telephone call to New York,
please.' He threw in a smile of encouragement. She
faltered, picked up a paper or two on her counter, and
set them aside. 'You want to call New York by telephone
and talk to somebody?' She said it just loudly enough
to reach everybody in the room. From the back corner
someone sniggered.

'Yes, that's exactly what I want.'

The clerk fiddled with her papers, her eyes downcast.

'You *do* have telephone connections?' pressed Rob.

'Y-yes,' she stammered. 'It says so on the adver-
tisement outside.'

'I remember,' he snapped, beginning to feel impatient. 'Talk directly to New York, Amsterdam, Paris—
isn't that what it says?'

'That's what it says.' Her voice went up-scale, ending
in a squeak of embarrassment. The middle-aged man at
the next corner, who had been eavesdropping, came over
and took the girl's place.

'What Margaret means to tell you,' he said confidentially, 'is that we can establish a connection by radio to Sint Maarten, and they can establish a connection by radio to San Juan, and *they* can establish a good connection to New York.'

'There's a *but* to this conversation?' asked Rob, beginning to see the humour of his situation.

'Well—yes,' the man said. 'After we establish all these connections, nobody seems to be able to hear anybody. And it costs a hundred guilders just to try!'

'Then is there some other way I can communicate with New York?'

'Oh yes, sir. We have an excellent postal service. If you airmail a letter today in Saba, it will be in New York in three days—two, if we are lucky. We pride ourselves on the speed and efficiency of our mail service.'

'And that's it? You don't even have cable service?'

'Ah—cable. Of course.' The man looked over his shoulder at the big wall clock. 'Van Steeden should be back from lunch in an hour. Mr Van Steeden is our only operator, you see. You would perhaps wish to write a cablegram?'

'I certainly would.' They exchanged grins, and again that graceful shrug of the shoulders. So what the hell, Rob told himself, the world doesn't run on New York time, or even New York habits. And one thing for sure is that this little—drama—needs to be investigated, and I'm going to do it. How much trouble can Harry get us into in just a couple or three weeks?

Rob Carlton, every inch the tycoon at leisure, accepted the invitation to share a desk, sat down with pencil and paper provided, and concocted this cable:

CARLTCABLE NY FOR SAITEMORE
INVESTIGATE TOP PRIORITY
CIRCUMSTANCES SURROUNDING BIRTH

EMERALD BLAKE LACKLAND APPROXI-
MATELY ELEVEN YEARS OLD PLACE
BIRTH UNKNOWN LIVED DURING FIRST
YEAR OF LIFE JONATHAN AND ANNE
BLAKE LONG ISLAND STOP NEXT
PRIORITY INVESTIGATE EXACT
WORDING WILL JACOB BLAKE FILED
HEMPSTEAD NEW YORK URGENT.

The clerk read the message over, displaying only a lifted eyebrow, counted the number of words, and collected the charge.

'And your address will be, Mr Carlton?'

'What?'

'Where shall we deliver the answer?'

'Oh, to me, care of Dr Laura Lackland, and I don't know the——'

'No need,' the man chuckled. 'Everybody knows Miss Laura. This message should be in New York in—perhaps—ten hours.'

Rob looked down at the bare counter in front of him, beset by many devils. *I need to know.* Surely, and how soon will everyone on the island know *what* I need to know? And which one of them will tell Laura? Strange, in spite of all my doubts, I still think of her as Lovely Laura. I ought to have my head examined. I ought to fly back to New York and find out for myself. I ought to—— God, I can't do that! No matter how bad the story is, I can't just walk off the stage and leave her behind!

A polite cough behind him indicated that someone else wanted to use the counter space. He moved aside apologetically, shoved his hands in his pockets, and walked outside. The heat struck him in the face. Not until that moment had he noted the ceiling fans that kept the office relatively cool.

Belle was sitting in the jeep, talking to a couple of friends standing on the sidewalk. A French patois, she was speaking. They were answering in Dutch. Rob shook his head. Crazy island, he told himself. Up ahead in the tiny square were two almost identical churches, one Catholic, the other Anglican. He climbed into the driver's seat, and had just started the motor when he heard a shrill female voice from across the street. 'Rob! Rob Carlton!' A diminutive blonde woman in shorts and absurdly high heels was waving to him. He sighed in disgust. 'As if the world doesn't have enough troubles!' he muttered.

'That lady a friend of you?' Belle enquired so casually that she overdid her lack of interest.

'I'm not sure,' he grumbled, rubbing the back of his neck, 'either about the *lady* part, or the *friend*.' And then, in a louder voice, 'Damn it, Stacey, I thought I told you to stay in New York!'

# CHAPTER FOUR

EMERALD was home by three-thirty in the afternoon. Laura cleaned her brushes and slipped out of her smock. She was still wearing her bikini. 'Hard day at school, love?' she asked.

Her answer was a hug and a very large smack of a kiss on her forehead.

'That bad, huh? Well, a glass of orange juice and some cookies might help. Climb up here.' The child was bubbling with excitement, her face exploding with happiness.

'We had races at recess today, Mama. Guess what?'

'OK, I give up. What?'

'Well, we had a three-legged race—you know, two people side by side with the middle legs tied together.'

'I remember. Did you win?'

Her daughter gave her a very baleful stare. 'I had to run with a *boy*—how about that?—with a boy!'

'They're not poisonous, love,' laughed Laura. 'In fact, they can be very useful.'

'Well, not Billy Delange. He fell down ten feet from the ribbon. We were in first place, and that dope fell down. Oh, I could have murdered him!'

'I don't think that would be a good idea,' Laura smiled. 'Although when I was your age I remember more than one boy I felt like murdering! Does your leg ache today?'

'Only a little bit. Nice cookies. Did Belle make them?'

'Well, what a lot of confidence you have in your mother! *I* made them, young lady. What do you have to say to that?'

'They're *still* nice, Mama. Where's Mr Carlton?'

'Gone into town with Belle, dear. He had to make a long-distance telephone call, or something like that. He's a very important man, you know, with lots of business to transact.'

'I hope he stays a while. I like him.' The last cookie on the plate disappeared, almost swallowed whole.

'Get your bathing suit on, Emerald,' said Laura. 'We'll swim together today, and do your exercises.'

'Nice, Mama! I like *you*, too.'

'Thank you, dear. I come in third place, just behind cookies and Mr Carlton?'

'Mama!' The child gave her a disgusted look, climbed down and ran, leaving a vacuum behind her. So much love, Laura thought, so much devotion she has to give. And she likes Mr Carlton. I don't know whether I do or not—but I wish he would stay a while. Just to give me a chance to find out how I really feel, of course. He's a very—interesting man.

She was already in the pool when Emerald came out. The child wasted no time, diving in head-first from the side. Once in the water, all the little girl's awkwardness disappeared. She swam like a fish. The two of them played at splash and duck and dodge, and all the other little games a pair can concoct. Half an hour later they heard the jeep. It was hard not to. Birds fluttered up from the trees in fright as the mechanical wreck banged its way down the driveway. Laura swam over to the poolside nearest the kitchen.

'Everything all right, Belle?'

The kitchen door was opened from the inside. 'Everything fine, Missy. Hot in Bottom, like always. I see fifteen, twenty people, all say give regards to Miss Laura.'

'You mailed the letter to Mr Butler?'

'I did that.'

'Then we'll have some money in the bank pretty soon. And our quarterly allotment from the government in another week? We're rich, Belle!'

'If you say so, Miss Laura. We so rich, I bought steak for everybody tonight!'

'Hooray!' Emerald yelled from across the pool. 'Where's Mr Carlton?'

'He right behind me, baby. An' he brought somebody.' Belle's voice dropped clear to the cellar, leaving no doubt of her opinion. Laura swam slowly over to the pool ladder and rested there. In a moment, Rob Carlton appeared. He had taken the time to buy himself a flamboyant pair of local swimming trunks. They were the only things he wore, apart from a big smile. He stepped aside, and Laura caught her breath, then bit down hard on her lower lip.

'Laura—Dr Lackland,' said Rob. 'May I present an old—family friend from New York? This is Stacey Mantoff. I took the liberty of inviting Stacey along. Her room at Windwardside is not quite ready yet.'

She's not *old* enough, Laura concluded gloomily as she climbed up out of the pool. Stacey Mantoff was equipped with a pneumatic figure, hardly covered by the tiny bikini. Her long, straight, blonde hair was combed in a sheen of loveliness down her back, tied at her nape with a blue ribbon. What there was of the bikini was blue as well. Everything else was gleaming ivory.

'Of course she's welcome,' Laura forced herself to say. 'Would you care to swim? The pool is warm at this time of day.'

'I don't swim,' the woman returned. Her voice was high, and verged on the edge of shrillness.

'Well, I do,' declared Rob, and dived off the edge in mad pursuit of an elusive Emerald.

'My daughter Emerald,' Laura explained. 'They seem to have struck up a great friendship. Why don't you and I sit it out? Would you like something to drink?'

'Please. In the shade,' Stacey returned. 'I have to be careful of my skin.'

'And a good thing, too,' Laura agreed cheerfully. The only reason I don't is because I'm not smart enough, Miss Mantoff. One up for you! 'What do you drink? We have all sorts of juices.'

'Gin and tonic,' said Stacey as she sank into the chair with a sigh. 'It's so warm on this silly little island.'

'All the time,' Laura said, then passed drink orders on to Belle.

'What kind of name is that—Mantoff?' Belle grumbled. 'Why you ask she eat with us? She don't like us, you won't like her!'

'Now, Belle,' Laura soothed. She carried the tray, including her own iced tea, back to the poolside and settled in an adjacent chair.

'So what brings you to Saba, Miss Mantoff?' she asked politely.

The woman took three thirsty sips of her drink, then put it down. 'Cats and mice,' she said archly. 'Rob is *my* mouse. I try not to let him out of my sight.'

'He—you mean you're engaged?'

'You might say that. I've known Rob Carlton for years, my dear. He has a tendency to stray—you know how men are. So, when I heard about this little adventure, I thought I'd just pop along. Although I must confess I'd never have thought you to be *his* type. A female dentist—how quaint!' Stacey lay back in her chair as if the discussion had exhausted her.

'Well, it's a living,' muttered Laura. At closer examination, little Miss Mantoff wasn't standing up to her image. There were suspicious spots of black at the base of all that blonde hair!

'You needn't let it worry you.' Laura had required only twenty seconds to analyse what was going on. 'This is purely business.'

'Yes, but you have no idea how far these business tycoons will go to complete a deal,' Stacey returned. 'But I wasn't worried—not after seeing you, my dear.' How about a good punch in the mouth, would that bother you? Laura screamed inwardly. So that's what he's up to. If his appeal to logic doesn't work, he's going to try another approach! She was seething inside, but let none of it appear on the surface.

'I suppose you know all about Mr Carlton's business?' she asked.

'Yes, indeed. I'm a stockholder, you know. In a minor way, of course.'

'And what do you do back home in New York?' Laura didn't want to know, but the conversation must be kept going.

'Do?' Stacey gave her a very strange look. 'One doesn't have to *do* anything in particular. I have fun, travel——' She paused in mid-sentence. And watch the mousehole, Laura added mentally. If she's that good, why aren't they married?

It was almost as if the other woman were reading her mind. Rob caught sight of the two heads together in the shade, and was racing for the exit ladder. 'And of course I expect to be married in the spring,' Stacey hastened to add. Rob came trotting up to them, shaking water drops over everything.

'Stacey can't stay for dinner,' he said with flat finality. 'In fact, I think I'd better run her over to the hotel and see about a room.'

'Oh, but Rob...' The blonde was making a patently false protest. She got up immediately, and the pair of them walked off. 'I'll be back shortly,' he called over his shoulder.

\* \* \*

He was back before Laura had finished rearranging her thoughts. Emerald was drying off in the far corner of the pool area and Belle was busy in the kitchen. Laura, lost in a daydream where the Staceys of this world could never enter, was suddenly snatched up out of her chair and kissed with as much skill as enthusiasm.

'Don't,' she said weakly, meaning don't stop. Damn the man! It's not fair to womankind. And look at that smile! 'I wish you hadn't done that,' she said softly, out of Emerald's hearing.

'Why?' Rob shook his hair free, looking more like a latter-day pirate than a businessman.

Why? Because I liked it too much, that's why, she told herself fiercely. And I've no intention of telling you. Not at least until I know what you're up to, mister!

'You have obligations, and my daughter is watching,' she told him, trying to make it sound important.

'And you never let a man kiss you in front of your daughter?'

'I never let a man kiss me, period,' she returned.

'Come play with me!' Emerald shrieked. 'Mama's tired from working!'

'Supper!' Belle banged the bottom of a frying pan to announce the meal, and the three of them trooped in. The food was quickly demolished.

'You know, I think that's the best supper we've had in—oh, weeks,' said Emerald. 'Thank you, Belle.'

'Never mind that "thank you, Belle" business. You an' me is scooting to the bathtub right now.'

'Aw, I must be the cleanest kid on the island! I want to talk to Mr Carlton.'

'Another time, dear.' Laura exchanged hugs as the two of them went out, the debate quelled as soon as she had spoken. Across the table from her, Rob sipped at his coffee.

'I don't understand what's going on,' he said. 'Emerald is probably one of the richest children in America, and you're all barely making it, month to month.'

'What are you suggesting, Rob?' she asked warily.

'Why, I'm suggesting that you take some of her profits and use them to live it up.'

'Ah. I see.' Her own mug was empty, but she swirled it around and imitated a sip to give time to think.

'You don't care for that solution?'

'No, I guess I don't. In the first place, it's Emerald's money. I can support my daughter. When she's grown up, her future will be assured. True, I'm not doing well from time to time, but you have to remember that people working for the Peace Corps, even dentists, don't expect to become millionaires. After my contract runs out— oh, about two months from now—we'll look around for a practice, and be comfortable.'

'That's reason number one—it's Emerald's money.'

'Yes. Reason number two is more difficult to explain. I've seen a great many rich girls who turned out to be the worst sort of snob the world could expect. No manners, no feelings for others. I don't want that for Emerald. She's a very—sacred trust, to me. I want her to grow up normally, mix with other children both poor and rich, and come to appreciate life. As she gets older— seventeen, eighteen, perhaps, I mean to have her study business under the best tutors I can find. Then, when she's twenty-one—and that's only ten years from now— she'll be able to handle her own money without any guidance from me. That's the way I see things for my Emerald, not some wild, confusing life——'

'Like your own?'

'Who told you that?' Her eyes snapped with anger. Her own life was private, not to be dealt out to strangers like a deck of cards. Besides, she told herself uneasily, he wants something from us, and the less he knows about me the better.

'Nobody told me, Miss Prickly Pear. I have eyes to see. I made my own deductions. Would you believe it, Doctor, Carltonworld didn't even know you existed until I came down here. And neither did I.'

'It's a very big world, Carltonworld, isn't it?' Laura ducked her head into the shadows. This man knew too much about body language for any woman's good.

'Yes. Very big.' There was just a little touch of pride in his voice, as if he meant to add, 'And I built it!'

She tapped at the table nervously with her long, strong fingers. 'Then I don't understand how you can stay away from it so long.'

'It's run by a team,' he explained, 'not just by an individual. I have an important mission down here. And besides——'

'Besides what?'

'I haven't had a vacation in years. More years than I can count. I thought—during this trip to the big city——' Rob grinned at her so attractively that she couldn't resist a return smile. 'That's better. I thought I would like to combine business with vacation pleasure. Unfortunately, Stacey took the only vacancy available at the hotel rooms.' The sentence wasn't a question, but it ended up in the air as if it were one.

So, there you go, Laura, she told herself. Sitting here smiling at him over an empty coffee mug, while he does his best to get his nose under the tent. But then, we don't know what he's up to, do we? If he goes off someplace else we'll never know, until what he's doing comes banging down on top of us. Am I being clever, or stupid? Formal logic was never my best subject. And no, it has nothing to do with his damnable smile, or those masculine good looks. I'm too old to fall for *that* sort of nonsense. Aren't I? Lord, I really don't know, do I?

Make it heads or tails. She tossed a coin mentally in her mind. It came rattling down and stood on edge. She shook her head and let loose with one big long sigh.

'We'd be pleased to have you stay with us, Rob,' she said softly. 'That is, if you don't mind such restricted quarters or lack of creature comforts.'

He became his most expansive self. The smile was enough to decoy Ulysses. 'Wonderful!' he chuckled. 'I know I'll enjoy it. You won't object if I make one or two minor changes to keep in touch with my office, would you?'

'Minor?' she queried.

'Well, for example, I'd like to get a telephone in— temporarily, of course, and on my business expense account.'

'I don't mind, as long as they're only little things, but I—I'm not sure that the telephone company could get one installed in such a short time.'

'If they can't, they can't,' he shrugged. 'Although I *did* make some preliminary enquiries while I was downtown.'

'Did you now?' Laura's suspicions were aroused quickly. 'You were so sure of staying here?'

'Not at all,' he assured her grandly. 'In fact, I thought more than likely you'd give me my marching orders. But I like it here. And I like all of you.'

'I'm glad you like us, because we all like you, too.'

'*All* of you?'

Laura blushed and ducked her head, then gave herself a lecture. What a way for an almost-thirty to act! Straighten out and fly right, girl! He's got his *own* girl tucked away over at the hotel!

'To varying degrees, of course,' she qualified, doing her best to hide her smile.

'Of course,' Rob replied solemnly, and quickly changed the subject. 'I do believe that's a moon shining out there. Care to come and look?'

'We *do* have them pretty regularly. Is there something special about this particular one?'

'You'll never know until you try it.' Somehow, everything he said made sense, even though Laura knew it was strictly a come-on. She took his hand and clutched it tightly, desperately, until they were out by the swimming pool, when it slipped away from her, and ended up around her shoulders.

A tropical moon is like no other on earth. It always seems so close, so huge, so alive. And in the quarter of the sky that the moon had left, the stars gleamed bright and big. Funny thing, Laura told herself as she leaned back against his comforting shoulder, I've been down here for almost a year and I never noticed that about the moon before! Nor the stars!

Perched as they were on the outer lip of the plateau, they could see the moonlit path cut across the white-tipped waves, almost a thousand feet below them. And, if one strained, and imagined just a little, there were a few gleams of light on the neighbouring island of 'Statia—Sint Eustatius, to be formal about it.

'There's a falling star,' Rob whispered in her ear.

'That's an airliner coming into Sint Maarten for a landing,' Laura corrected in an enormously superior tone. He retaliated by nipping the lobe of her ear. She yelped and turned around towards him—which led to everything else that followed. She blamed herself. After all, he already had one arm around her, and when she turned his other joined the fray, naturally. Which left Laura trapped up against his solid chest. Not that she minded that part of it. In fact, she turned her head to lay her cheek flat against the smooth silk of his shirt, and it was altogether nice—the sort of thing one might well substitute for an after-dinner liqueur. And, if she shivered, it might well be blamed on the coolness of the breeze at that altitude, mightn't it? It was a good argument to have with oneself, and it left Laura the option of judging herself as a mighty cool lady.

But the rest of it was definitely *not* cool. Rob tilted her head up with a finger under her chin, his lips came slowly down on hers, and all her controls broke down.

His lips barely touched, caressed, lifted, then came down again. The second time it was as if a bolt of lightning had struck her. There was more to him than lips, warm, tasting, teasing, and she could not stop her arms from going up around his neck, or her hips from swaying forward until they were almost glued to his. Nor could she still the urgent excitement that swelled up from the pit of her stomach to invade and control her mind.

Rob hesitated for a split second, then pulled her tighter, closer. His hands roamed her back, from the curve of her hips to the spread of her shoulders. Her breasts flattened against him. She went up on her toes to maintain the contact. It was like floating ten feet above the water, with star-bursts showering behind her closed eyelids, and fireworks chasing each other on the horizon. Then his lips relaxed.

'Wow!' he muttered.

'Wow, indeed!' she gasped. 'They don't teach that course in dental school!'

'Maybe it was an accident,' he said solemnly. 'We'd better try it again to make sure.'

'Tell me what to do,' sighed Laura. Instead, he showed her. His head came down again, his lips sealed her off from all the rest of the world, and she was a free-floating star herself, shooting off into the unknown cosmos with only Rob for a guide. At which point the kitchen door slammed.

'Are you kissing my mother?' An irate little girl, dragging her favourite bear by the foot, glared at them. Rob sighed as he broke contact and set Laura down on her feet. She staggered a little, and might have fallen had he not still been holding her. She hid her head against his chest. Let *him* explain it, she thought. I don't have the courage—or the breath.

'You know, I believe I am,' he agreed.

The child considered the situation. 'Grandpa kissed Mama.'

'That must have been nice.'

'But he didn't do it the way you're doing it.'

'Didn't he? Well, grandfathers are pretty old.'

'That's true. And he wasn't as tall as you are, either.'

'And nobody else has ever kissed your mother?' queried Rob.

'Well, me and Belle. I mean—Belle and I—we kiss her a lots. Men, I mean. Was it nice?'

'I think it was very nice. Extremely nice, for that matter. Should I have asked your permission first?'

'We-ell.' Emerald drawled the word out, considering. 'No, I guess it's all right. But you'd better be careful about Belle. She gets very uptight about kissing and things, especially where Mama is concerned. She's likely to ask you what—what——' the child's forehead wrinkled in a struggle to remember, then she smiled '—what your intentions are?'

'My intentions?' Rob paused solemnly. 'I think my intention is to kiss your mother again.'

Emerald skipped over to one of the lounge chairs and sat down. 'OK, I'll watch. I bet there's a lot I could learn about this stuff.'

'Now wait just a darn minute, you two!' Laura had finally regained control of herself, and was breathing normally. 'I have something to say about all this.' She wrestled herself free from Rob's gentle arms and stepped back a pace or two.

'There now,' he said dolefully to the girl, 'you spoiled the mood. Now she doesn't want to play any more.'

'In that case, you can come tell me a bedtime story!' Emerald shouted gleefully.

And there go two of a kind, mused Laura as the pair of them joined hands and went off into the house. She wandered over by the hedge that separated office from house. The smell of hibiscus and lemon was almost overwhelming. She leaned against the bole of the single palm tree that had sprung up in the middle of the hedge, watched the moon glide over the peak of the mountain, and listened to the subdued sound as Rob told a tale and her daughter giggled.

He loves children. I wonder if he has any of his own. I wonder if there's a family, waiting for him, watching out of their windows for—damn it, Laura, get a hold on your imagination! Disgusted with herself, she turned her back on the moonlight and stalked into the kitchen. Belle was busy at the sink.

'Another cup of coffee, love?'

'Thank you, Belle, I guess I could use some stimulant. The whole world seems to be—uneasy—these days.'

'Ain't the whole world. Just one stubborn girl think she too old for the matin' game, that's what!'

'Belle! What a thing to say!' exclaimed Laura. 'I'm not an eighteen-year-old, you know.'

'I know, Missy. When you was eighteen and oughta be playing, you was working and goin' to college at the same time, and then after that come Emerald. You never *been* young, girl. Never been! Always big responsibilities for such a little pair shoulders!'

'I promised Anne, Belle—you know that. *She* looked after me when I was a baby, and I promised to do the same for Emerald. Besides, it wasn't all *that* much work.

You were always there, and Grandpa helped, and old Mr Blake, he paid half of all the expenses.'

'Which you worked hard to pay him back, didn't you?'

'Well—so I worked to pay him back. Isn't that what a person's supposed to do? I never would have finished dental school without his help—and yours. And I haven't paid *you* back yet, have I?'

'Me? Lordy, girl, you don't hafta pay me! I had all the fun in the world! You was the daughter I couldn't have!'

'I know, Belle. I'm sorry, I shouldn't have said that. You're family—you always have been. See? I've been a lucky girl. *I* had *two* mothers—you and Anne. And an extra grandfather, Mr Jacob. And my own Gramps—so why do I feel like crying?'

''Cause what I told you, Missy. You missed out on bein' young. And now here comes a man can make for you all that young you never was, and you fightin' it, don't you?'

'Well, really!' protested Laura. 'You don't think I'm going to just jump in his arms, do you? He's only here for a little time, and then he'll be gone. And he's got his own woman on the side!'

'And that's just what I think, Missy. Jump in his arms. Say goodbye to them doubts. So he only stays a little time. So what? You learn more in a little time than most women learn all their lives. And who knows—maybe you enjoy yourself while you doin' it. No? Hush up you tears. Dry up the eyes. Here he come.'

'I'm not disturbing you, am I?' Rob's presence was a long shadow over the discussion. Laura looked up at him out of the corners of her eyes. Jump in his arms? she thought. I've already done that! What else could I do?

'No. We were just talking family,' she told him. 'Please come and sit down, Mr—er—Rob. I was having a second cup of coffee. Would you like something stronger?'

'I wouldn't mind.' He pulled up a chair, tested its strength, and sat down gingerly. 'What do you have?'

'We got white rum,' Belle replied. 'If you don't like that, we got brown rum.'

'I'll have it.' He was staring at her. Laura wished he wouldn't do that. There seemed to be no place to hide. Belle faded out of sight into the living-room, and came back with a glass, to which she added ice. She set it in front of him on the table and disappeared again. Rob was still staring at her, paying no attention to the glass. Laura looked around desperately, but Belle was no longer her safe haven.

'Have what?' she whispered.

He leaned across the table. 'Anything I can get, Miss Laura Lackland. Anything I can get. What's on offer?'

'Well, not me!' she replied shrilly. 'Just drinks. Just— there in front of you. That's all! Stop staring at me!'

'Does it make you nervous?'

'You know darned well it does, Rob Carlton. What would your wife say about that?'

'I don't have a wife. I've never had a wife. I don't have any children. I don't have any mistresses—well, at the present moment, I mean.'

Oh, don't you now? she thought bitterly. What about Stacey? 'Am I supposed to qualify as your mistress?'

'I didn't say it, Laura, but if you feel like you'd want the position, it's open.' And that gorgeous smile. Damn the man!

'I'm not interested.' She banged the table for emphasis, and only managed to spill hot coffee over her hand. 'Darn you, see what you've made me do!'

Rob picked up her slightly burned hand. 'There now. Let me kiss it better.' She snatched the hand away, and tucked it behind her back.

'No, you won't,' she said grimly. 'I know what you're up to.' Yes, I do, she thought. First you kiss my hand, then you kiss my lips, then I fall to pieces again as I did outside, and before I know it we're both in one bed and—— Oh God, I want that so badly!

It was a struggle, but she managed. 'You stay on your side of the table and I'll stay on mine,' she stated flatly. 'And perhaps you'd be so good as to tell me just why you've come to Saba to get Emerald's proxies.'

'I thought we weren't going to do that until both you and Emerald could listen?'

'I've changed my mind—that's my prerogative. Haven't you ever known a woman who changed her mind?'

'Regularly,' he sighed. 'So all right, I'll explain. But I need something. May I go out and come back without disturbing your personal space?'

'Just get it,' snapped Laura. He grinned at her, got up, and walked out. Moments later he was back with his briefcase. Laura watched him warily as he unsnapped it. He can't be a real tycoon, she assured herself. If he were he'd have a fancy case, not that black leather affair! The thought gave her a little strength.

'Here it is,' he said, laying a box on the table. 'The top of our line—the Little Mother doll. Bound to make us a fortune, according to all our surveys.' His big fingers fumbled with the fastenings. The doll he took out caught her breath—about twenty inches long, with long silver hair, a carefully crafted face, and a ballgown that would give any woman pause.

'It does something, of course?' she asked warily.

'Of course.' He stood it up and showed her a pair of switches on the back. 'Say something, Laura.'

'I—hello,' she managed.

'I don't understand,' the doll answered.

'Oh, dear lord, a conversational doll? I don't believe it!'

'Better than that,' chuckled Rob as he handed her a piece of paper. 'Read that sentence slowly when I nod my head.' He fingered a switch in the doll's back and nodded. The words on the paper didn't seem to make sense, but she read them anyway. When she was finished he moved the switch again.

'And what was that all about?' Curiosity had got the better of her.

'That code you read has been fed into the little computer inside the doll, and now *your* voice has been registered. Yours, and yours only. Now, when I throw this other switch, talk to her again. Ready?'

'Hello, I'm Laura,' said Laura obediently.

'Hello, Laura,' the doll responded. 'I'm Mary.'

Laura sat and stared, amazed. Rob was making hand signals to her. 'How are you, Mary?' she asked.

'I'm fine. How are you, Laura?' Rob flipped the switch in the doll's back and laid her down on the table.

'As you see,' he chuckled, 'the doll lives. It will answer only to your voice, and has about seven stock conversational bits. You happened on two good ones at first crack. What do you think?'

'I'm flabbergasted,' she replied honestly. 'Absolutely astounded!'

'Do you think a little girl might like a doll like that?'

'I—I'm sure her mother would,' Laura said slowly. 'That's who buys the things, isn't it?'

His face fell. 'And you don't think the child would?'

'Oh—I don't know, Rob. I'm no expert. I rather expect a child would be pleased for the first couple of days, and then when she was through astounding her friends—

or when they all had one—the flavour would wear off. How long does the battery last?'

'We anticipate twenty user-hours. That means twenty hours of conversation. What do you think?'

'I don't know,' she said simply. 'But you didn't bring that all the way down here just to astound Emerald—or me—did you?'

'No, I didn't. But this *is* the core of the problem. Laura, how much do you know about making toys?'

'Nothing. Or next door to it,' she answered.

'To keep it simple, then, most toys are designed by American staffs and built in foreign countries. In our case, we have two factories in Thailand, and one each in Taiwan and Hong Kong.' He anticipated her question. 'Labour costs, Laura. They're so much lower in these Third World areas.'

'So, all right, you still haven't come to the problem.'

'No, I haven't. As you might guess, Carltonworld is engaged in a big advertising campaign with this doll. That's what sells toys, by the way—advertising. Our board expects the Little Mother to bring in over sixty per cent of our profits for next year.'

'And?'

'I've recommended that we take it off the market. The board isn't happy about that. They want not only to market the doll, but also to get rid of me. That's why I need your—Emerald's—proxies.'

'But why, Rob? Why not market it!' queried Laura. 'I don't personally think it's a good toy, but millions will. What's the problem?'

'The problem is this, Laura. With our factories widespread and overseas, we don't have much control over what actually goes into the doll. So here we have a triple feature. The doll's face is painted with lead-based paint. Little kids have the habit of kissing—and even licking—their dolls. Lead paint is poisonous. Secondly, we prescribed that the doll be stuffed with sterilised cotton. Instead, the factories used cotton waste. And third— well, here. Put your finger right here.'

He was pointing towards the doll's midriff. Laura did as he asked. 'Push.' She did.

'Good lord, I think I cut my finger!' she reported, looking at its tip.

'Yes. Mistake number three. The computer parts were supposed to be enclosed in a completely round, sealed plastic ball. Our people discovered they couldn't get enough stability from the design, so they changed to aluminum. And that's what you stuck your finger on. Add them all up. Wrong paint, improper stuffing, and an injury risk from the internal mounting. So I recommended that we cut our losses, scrap the whole thing, and try again some other time.'

'And your board?' she asked.

'They know that the child safety people will murder us in the United States, so they agree not to use it at home. But they want to export it—without warning— to all the other countries we serve. By doing that, they can still make enough to cover our costs.'

'Why, that's—that's dishonest!' she protested.

'No, not really. That's business.'

'If I ran *my* business that way, half the population on this island would have a toothache. That's dishonest.'

'And you've never known a dentist who did a shoddy job, used the cheapest filling material, overcharged?'

Laura held up her hands in surrender. 'All right, all right! I think I'm getting a headache.'

'Then you'll sign the proxies?'

'I'll think it over,' she promised. 'And I'll talk it over with Emerald. What would Jacob have done?'

'You knew Mr Blake?'

'Of course. What would *he* have done?'

'Who knows?' sighed Rob. 'He wouldn't have had these problems, because he didn't know beans about toys. But you'll——'

'I *said* I'll think it over,' she mumbled. 'Right now, I'm going to take a shower and go to bed. Tomorrow is Friday, and it will be a long day!'

'For me, too,' he said. 'I'll be gone most of the day. Business, of course.'

'Of course.' Stacey business? her mind enquired. Laura got up from her chair slowly and walked towards the door. Whether by chance or miscalculation, her hand trailed across Rob's bare arm. He said nothing, did nothing, as she squeezed by him and went down the corridor. Belle was on the lookout, and entered the kitchen as Laura went out. As Laura headed towards the shower, she could hear the muted tones of the two of them, back in the kitchen together.

Laura was in a daze as she turned on the shower water and unbound her hair. Do it up good, she told herself. Shower and shampoo and think. Of course Rob was right; it would be dishonest to sell the dolls to anyone. But if you tell him tomorrow and sign the proxies, he'll be gone faster than you can say Jack Robinson. And then what happens to all those ethereal dreams, Dr Lackland? So you have to be dishonest, too. Stall him. Tell him you're still thinking about it. Right!

With renewed energy she scrubbed and shampooed, rubbed and smoothed, brushed and combed, and all the while, in her mind, Rob was watching. The idea bothered her. Never in her life had she had to measure up to other women as a woman. Nobody in dental school cared if your hair glistened, if your stomach was flat, your waist small, your hips well rounded. None of her patients cared if her breasts, hidden beneath the eternal white coat, were firm and full. Nobody cared, not until now. She wiped steam from the mirror and took a good look, not realising that her hands had been shaping and testing all these places while she thought. She snatched them away, grabbed up a towel and her robe, and ran for her bedroom.

# CHAPTER FIVE

IT WAS raining when Rob came to breakfast, the first rain, except for the regular noonday shower, that he had seen since he'd arrived on the island. The three women looked gloomy, settled around the kitchen table.

'It's the start of the rainy season,' Laura explained. 'Forty days and forty nights on and off—or longer. Everything stops on Saba in the heavy rains.'

'Everything but the school,' Emerald complained. 'You can sit and enjoy. I have to go out in it!'

'I'll drive you to school,' he offered, astonishing even himself. The irony struck him immediately—Rob Carlton, the Terror of the Toy World, offering to drive a little girl to school in the rain! 'I hope word of this doesn't get around New York,' he whispered. Laura heard.

She lifted her head and sat up straight. There was a gleam in her eye. Laughter? The damn woman was laughing at him! For a moment he had his usual reaction—anger. And then he looked around the little homey kitchen, the laughing faces, the love—and started to laugh at himself.

'Are you going to drive me to school, honest?'

'Cross my heart and hope to be a Scout.'

'You're silly. I don't have time to talk about rain.' But the smile she offered was worth the trouble.

'Come on, Lady Emerald,' he ordered.

They waded out to the jeep, which was squatting disconsolately in a puddle of water. There was even water

83

inside, almost an inch of it on the floorboards. 'You left the drainplug in,' Emerald said accusingly.

'Did I? I had hoped the thing would float. Where is it?'

'Right under your feet. That little nut-thing on the floor. It screws out.' And it did. Water gurgled and ran, and in a moment more was running out than was coming in. Rob settled himself into the poncho which Belle had provided, crossed his fingers, and tried the key. The old engine grumbled, fired, and thundered at him. It was a matter of less than fifteen minutes, running up to the schoolhouse and coming back. The poncho had protected his upper body, but his trouser legs, below the knees, were soaked. Belle and Laura were still in the kitchen.

'More coffee? You got wet, man,' the old lady laughed. 'Ain't gonna do no harm—warm clean rain. You get used to it.' He accepted the towel she passed him, and dried his hair. The steaming coffee was just the thing.

'No more customers this morning, Doctor?' She looked up at him and smiled.

'No customers. When it rains on Saba everything stops—except the school system. Who wants to get a tooth fixed in weather like this?'

'And besides, you're tired?' He didn't need an answer. She seemed to droop, like a blossom beaten down by the rain. She sucked thirstily at her mug.

'Why not take a nap?' he suggested. 'I've business to attend to—down at Bottom. So you have no guests to entertain, no teeth to drill——'

Laura shook her head. 'There's always something else to be done,' she sighed. 'I've a thousand miles of painting to finish before the end of the month, and all I seem to do is dabble.'

'Have you given any thought to the proxies I asked for?'

'I've given it thought, but I don't have an answer for you,' she said softly. 'What would happen if you didn't get our proxies? Could we come to the meeting and vote for ourselves?'

'I suppose you could, Laura. As Jacob's heir, Emerald is entitled to vote, I think. But you would have to establish your identity before the vote.'

'I'm still thinking.' Her voice was low and warm, and Rob Carlton would have given half his business to be able to snatch her up and take her to bed with him for the whole day—but the wary look in her eyes convinced him it wasn't time for that yet. And maybe never. It depended on the answers to his cabled questions.

'Then let me at least leave you some information.' Laura gestured towards the table next to her. He piled it high with pamphlets, and almost broke out laughing at the heavy sigh from behind him.

'I'll be in the studio, Belle.' Laura stood up and stretched, and wandered out into the hall.

'I call you if any patients come,' Belle called after her. She turned around towards Rob. 'That girl work too hard. Don't never take no vacations—work, work, work. You gonna drive to Bottom in this rain?'

'I guess I'll have to,' he chuckled. 'I don't think I can fly down there.'

'Not funny, man,' she grunted as she started to collect the dishes. 'Days like this, even the birds walk. You be sure you careful and slow on the cliff road, no?'

Rob remembered it vividly—that winding narrow shelf, suspended over a thousand-foot drop. 'I'll be careful. What time does Emerald get out of school?'

'Three o'clock.'

'I'll be back in time to pick her up.'

He stood up, reaching for the poncho again, but Belle laid a hand on his arm, stopping him. The strength of her grip startled him. The muscles in her arms stood out. This woman might be old, but she's not soft, he told himself. Now what?

'What you doin' about Emerald?' she asked suspiciously.

'Just picking her up from school, Belle.'

'That's not what I mean, and you know it. What you *doin'* about Emerald? Tell me honest, man. These girls, both of them my children. You hear me? Anybody hurts my girls, I gonna do somethin', and you ain't gonna like it.'

He looked down at her determined face. 'And I'll bet I wouldn't,' he confessed. 'Belle—I don't ever expect to do anything that would hurt Emerald. Anything. I've never dealt with children, but I like this one. As for Laura——'

'You don't gotta tell me about you and Missy. I can see that in you eyes, man. That don't make me mad. She need some man—some good man. But if you hurts either one of them—my papa was *obeah*. You understand?'

'*Obeah*? Witchman?'

'Maybe. Hard work to translate—more than witch, less than devil. Just you mind what I tell you. Don't hurt my children!'

'I—I'd better get going,' said Rob hastily. 'I'll be back by supper time.'

Belle glowered at him as he went out the door. It gave him an uneasy feeling, as if a single eye were following along behind him, watching every step he took, boring into the back of his neck and into his mind. It wasn't until the rain slashed into his face that he was able to shrug off the thought.

\*     \*     \*

Laura spent the rest of the day in her studio. It was a small room at the back of the house, constructed almost entirely of glass, affording plenty of bright tropical light, when there was any. Today there was plenty of light, but the rain hammered and rattled at roof and side windows, and gave her the feeling of working ten fathoms down. She had made little progress with the work at hand for the past days. Something else had been hanging on the fringe of her mind, until she put her two commissions away against the wall and worked with jerky energy on something she neither wanted nor needed to do. She heard the jeep when it came back, its rattling passage more than capable of overcoming the incessant beat of the rain.

She could hear Rob's deep baritone, spiced by Emerald's high excited answers. Something was on, she could tell. They thundered into the house and came down the corridor to the closed door of the studio. Laura could hear the debate through the thin door.

'No! You can't go in there,' the child said abruptly. 'That's the rule. When Mama's painting, nobody goes in there. Nobody. Not for anything!'

'Not even to share our secret?'

'Not even. Mama says she'll blister my bottom if I interrupt.'

'But your mother could hardly blister *my* bottom, could she?'

'Well—maybe not. But I don't worry about you, I just worry about me!'

'So we'll go in together. She won't know which one of us to hit first.'

'All right, you two conspirators!' Laura put her brush and palette down, drew a cloth cover over the painting on the easel, and opened the door. 'What is it that's so important?'

They stood side by side, holding hands, dripping wet and trying to look innocent—and hopeful. 'Have you finished painting for today?' asked Emerald, just the slightest bit hesitant.

Rob jiggled the child's hand to get her attention. 'How many times has your mother blistered your bottom, young lady?'

Emerald looked up at him, weighing him. 'Not ever,' she admitted. 'But she *says* she will, and I don't want to take the chance that this is the day.'

'Come in, for goodness' sakes. Don't just stand there and jabber at each other,' Laura chided. 'The sooner you get in, the sooner you'll get out. And I have some work to finish.' Did I sound too impatient? Too much like a shrew? she thought. I don't really have to finish anything. I'm just doodling!

They came in together, Emerald's small brown hand in Robert's large one, looking very much like Brutus and friend. Check to see if there are daggers in those other hands, Laura thought.

It was the first time anyone outside the family had penetrated this forbidden ground. A baker's dozen paintings, half unframed, lined the walls. Another half-dozen unfinished canvases leaned against the walls in no apparent order. Rob made a slow round, measuring each painting carefully, then moving on.

'I like the style,' he commented. 'These are a great deal better than the ones I've seen in exhibitions in New York. You never did paint like this in the old days.'

'I was too young in the old days,' said Laura simply. His head snapped up, eyes following every emotion on her face. She forced herself to stand still. He turned back to the display, searching out one of the incomplete ones on the floor. Pinned to one corner of the painting were a series of charcoal drawings, three watercolour sketches, and half a dozen colour photographs.

'Is this the way you do your portraits?' asked Rob.

'Not always, but the Senator just wouldn't sit still. I finally told him it wasn't worth the trouble—so we compromised with what you see.'

'And you'll paint from these sketches and pictures.'

'I paint from my mind,' she snapped. 'I'm not into photo reproductions.'

He could see he had touched on a sore spot, and backed away from the paintings. In front of the easel he paused, his hand reaching up for the cloth cover. 'May I look at this? Work in progress, I suppose?'

Laura wanted very desperately to refuse permission. Her paintings always revealed as much of herself as of the subject. But she fumbled for the words too long. The cloth came off, and he whistled.

'That's Mr Carlton,' said Emerald in a hushed voice, then giggled. 'Four of him!'

'Will the real Rob Carlton please stand,' he said in a strangled voice. 'Is that how you see me?'

'I don't know,' Laura admitted. 'If I knew, I'd be certain, wouldn't I?' She moved over to his side to re-examine her work. It had been done hurriedly, with jerky strokes and strong colours. The background was a sporadically lit area, some comfortable Regency living-room. Around a circular, highly polished, table were four figures. The first was a standing man with a rounded stomach, a high forehead, a stern expression, using a quill pen as a pointer. The second was a man reclining at the table, well dressed in the fashion of the 1800s but wearing an eye-patch over his left eye, and a sly grin on his face. The third, standing at the end of the table was a tall uniformed man with bare sword upraised. And, in front of him, sprawled with long legs out before him towards the fire, a gracious young dandy with a magnificent smile, tapping the table with his quizzing glass. All of them wore Rob Carlton's face.

'How about the surprise?' Emerald insisted.

Laura was tired, impatient. Rob was responsible, but Emerald suffered. 'Don't chew your braids,' she snapped, and instantly regretted it. She held out her arms and the child ran across and leaped up at her.

'Rob picked me up at the school,' she said excitedly, 'and he met all the other teachers and all the other kids, and he drove me home!'

'That was very nice of him, but I don't think you should call him Rob. Mr Carlton, dear.'

'But he said I could, and he gave me a present!' Emerald lifted up her wrist. A lovely little watch adorned it.

'Oh, you shouldn't have done that,' Laura said sadly. 'It must have been very expensive.'

'Rob—Mr Carlton doesn't care, Mama. He's got lots of money!'

'Emerald, your face is dirty. Why don't you run into the bathroom and give it a wash?' She watched until the child was out of hearing distance. 'And that, Mr Carlton, is just the sort of lesson I don't want Emerald to learn.' Her face twisted in an emotion he could not define.

'I'm not ashamed of my money, Laura.' His voice had that deadly cold tone used in the boardroom, where careers could be ended by a few sharp words from Robert Carlton.

'I don't ask you to be ashamed, Mr Carlton. I'm sure you've worked hard for everything you have, and deserve the enjoyment of it. But Emerald is my daughter. I ask that you respect what I want her to learn.'

'Dammit, Doctor, I thought you'd be happy about it! I wanted to do it. Are you sure she's your daughter?'

'And just what does *that* mean?'

'Nothing,' he sighed. 'I'm sorry I brought it up.'

'Look here, Mr Carlton. Don't think I'm isolating my daughter from the world down here. We've lived in

Boston, in an urban environment. We've lived near Hartford in a rural environment, and now, for a year, we're living on Saba. I want Emerald to learn what each of these places has to teach her. And among the things Saba teaches is that one can live perfectly happily without all the materialism that sparks the world. I think you mean well, but it doesn't change the circumstances. While we're on Saba, I don't want you to give my daughter expensive gifts. And now, if you'll excuse me, I must find my bathing suit. Emerald needs her exercises.'

'In the pouring rain?'

'As long as it's not a thunderstorm, it hardly makes a difference. The water in the pool comes from last week's rain. This new deluge might be a degree cooler, but it's not important. Emerald's exercise schedule is rigid. If we follow it to the letter all this year, by next she may be walking as easily as any other twelve-year-old.'

'All right—I give up. I will positively not give *Emerald* any more expensive gifts.' Before she could move, Rob leaned down and dropped a kiss on the tip of her nose. She froze for a second, then rubbed the spot with her fingers.

'Oh, you——' she muttered as she swept by him and into her adjacent bedroom. He watched her sway down the hall. A dentist with a mission in life? A con woman trying to do *somebody* out of a fortune? Or just what he had thought that first night? Talented, concerned, lovely Laura? One part of his mind wanted an early report from New York; the other part hoped he would never hear from his people, ever. And what the hell way is that for an executive to be? he asked himself. What kind of a decision-maker are you, anyway?

It rained off and on throughout the whole weekend. Rob spent much of his time with Emerald, talking, playing, explaining. There were also a number of semi-secret conferences with Belle. Laura watched it out of the corner of her eye as she continued on her regular weekend schedule.

There were two dental emergencies, one a little boy in a bicycle accident. 'The tooth might be saved,' Laura told them all at lunch. 'It's one of his first adult molars, and that's important. It's loose, but I've supported it, and that's all that can be done. The old man? An abscess—very painful. I lanced it, put him on penicillin, and told him to come back in three days. That whole tooth area is in trouble, and I may have to do a root canal.'

The rest of her time was divided faithfully between her studio and Emerald, which threw her into contact with Rob. It was back to Rob again after that painful afternoon. I'm not one to hold a grudge, she told herself. I'm sure it was all an accident, wasn't it? He really wouldn't be trying to buy my daughter's affection, would he? Well, would he? She didn't like the vibrations that went with her own answer. He was going out of his way to be with Emerald, no doubt about it!

By the end of the second week they were all back on a first-name basis, and he had integrated himself into their family ways and schedules. On Saturday, after Laura's last patient had left, he came out into the dental office, with Emerald glued to his side. 'I have to go somewhere called Fort Bay,' he announced. 'How about a guide and a Cook's tour?'

'It's almost noon,' said Laura quietly as she put her tools into the gas-heated steam sanitiser. 'There's nothing at Fort Bay except the Customs House, you know. I doubt that——'

'But, Mama, it's ship day,' Emerald pleaded.

'Ship day?' Rob looked back and forth between the two of them.

'Tourist ships,' Laura explained. 'They take cruises around the islands. Saba is included, although hardly anyone stops off here.' He looked totally confused. She slipped out of her white coat and took pity on him. 'Come along, Robert. You'll see what we mean.' She took him by the arm and led him out into the garden. Belle, who surely must be telepathic, met them at the kitchen door with a lunch basket.

'Got no restaurants by Fort Bay, man. Don't want you should lose a whole meal.' The single gold tooth sparkled. So did her eyes. 'An' you be careful and treat my girl good, mister!'

'Oh, I'll treat Emerald with all good care,' he returned.

'Don't mean no Miss Emerald,' Belle told him in a husky whisper that could be heard throughout the house. 'You knows what I mean, man!' She managed, by stretching up on the tips of her toes, to pat his cheek gently.

'What was that all about?' asked Laura as they went out to the jeep. Rob helped her into the seat, although her long legs made help unnecessary.

'I haven't the slightest idea. Sometimes Belle—leaves me confused. Has she been with you long?'

'So long that I don't honestly remember when she came,' Laura returned. 'She was with Grandfather Lackland when Anne and I went to live with him. I don't even remember when that was. Isn't that strange? I meet people all the time who claim they can remember when they were two or three years old. I can't remember a thing before I was five—in fact, my first clear memory is of the day we drove up to Gramps' house and he came running out and gave us a big hug. Lord, he was so—tall! Like a giant.'

'They sound like good memories,' said Rob, patting her hand. It was the first reminder, and it embarrassed her. When they had left the dental office she had taken his hand, and still held it. More than held. Their fingers were intertwined, and Laura was reluctant to lose the contact. Robert, she thought. I like that better than Rob. Rob sounds like an underworld *capo* who specialises in banks. Robert. *My* Robert! The idea so overwhelmed her that she sank back in the seat and her face turned pale.

It was a preposterous idea. Probably that was what made it so acceptable. She repeated it a couple of times to herself. *My Robert. My Robert.*

'What are you up to? Your cheek is puffing in and out.'

She looked over at him and smiled. After all, he'd probably run for the airport if he knew what she was thinking! 'I nibbled on a breadstick between patients,' she explained. 'There's a little piece stuck behind my wisdom tooth. I really need to see a dentist!'

He returned her smile. 'So, why don't you?'

'They scare me to death,' she admitted wryly. 'That drilling noise drives me bonkers. I'm a real coward.'

'Yes, I can see you must be.' He sounded so solemn that she looked up quickly, and caught those eyes within inches of hers. They were filled with laughter. Emerald took that unfortunate moment to come bustling out of the house, carrying a scarf for Laura's hair. Unfortunate? thought Laura. Why did I think that? He was about to kiss me again. I'm sure of it—and then—well, it isn't my daughter's fault that he stopped in mid-stream, is it?

Laura traded Emerald a kiss for a scarf, and tied her hair. The jeep was old, battered, and very open. Riding in a vehicle like that required short hair or braids or— a polka-dot scarf. She had to giggle at that. The dots on her scarf matched those on the canvas top of the vehicle. And the great tycoon had added streamers to each of its corners. So he is alive and well, not just a boardroom executive! she told herself. 'Drive on, James—er—Robert,' she commanded.

'Which direction?' he asked mildly as he backed the vehicle, turned around, and headed up the drive.

'Well, if you want a Cook's tour,' she reflected, 'I suppose we ought to turn right. For just a few hundred feet.'

It doesn't take much time to tour an island where the four communities exist in a semicircle around the shoulder of a volcano. The Mountain actually had a name, Laura was forced to admit. Mount Scenery peaked at two thousand eight hundred feet.

'Upper Hell's Gate is up there.' She had stopped them in a bypass a bare eighth of a mile from home. A long flight of stairs led from the road in the direction she was pointing. 'Upper Hell's Gate is the same as Lower Hell's Gate, but there's more of it, and it's higher.'

'Yes, I can see that,' said Rob cautiously. 'How do we drive up there?'

'We don't,' she chuckled. 'It's at the head of those stairs. A hundred and fifty steps up. Shall we climb? Emerald will wait for us in the car.'

He was grinning at them both as he answered. 'Oh no, we can't *possibly* leave Emerald alone. It looks like Lower Hell's Gate, you say?'

There's so much syrup in that voice, I wish I had a stack of pancakes, Laura told herself—then suppressed the giggle that went with it. 'Exactly.'

'Then you won't mind if we don't climb—a hundred steps, you said?'

'And fifty,' she reminded him.

'And fifty. Yes.' Rob shrugged his shoulders, and turned the car around. They were off up the hill towards Windwardside before the doleful look on his face evaporated.

'I suppose this place is built on the only flat land on the island?'

'It's true that Windwardside is *almost* flat,' she teased, 'but then, so is Bottom. Don't you remember?'

'Oh, I remember all right. Why don't I see more *men* around? Everywhere we go I see women, and more women.'

'There are a few men,' Laura told him. 'Some farmers, some fishermen, some businessmen. But—well, tourism was supposed to save Saba, and it hasn't happened. Most of the men work off-island. They work on the oil-rigs in Aden, Mexico, Nigeria—places like that. If they're lucky, they come home on vacation once a year. It's been this way since the 1930s, when the sugar market dropped out of sight. Before then, sugar was the mainstay of practically all the Caribbean islands. But I'd rather talk about something else. Did you notice what the women were doing?'

'No. Knitting?'

'Just what I expected of a man!' she lectured. 'No, they're doing what's called "Spanish Work". They take a square of good linen, and then by pulling out selected threads they create decorative designs, something like lace, only more delicate. They sell well. Look, there's the hotel over there, right on the edge of the cliffs.'

'Please don't remind me,' he laughed. 'Four rooms make a hotel? It looks beautiful on the outside, but those beds—you wouldn't believe—I swear they came over from Spain with Columbus.'

'Poor man,' she sighed with crocodile sympathy.

'Columbus didn't land here,' Emerald announced from the back seat. 'We had that in school, and——'

'So I made a small mistake,' groaned Rob. 'Give your teacher my apologies.' He waved over at the cliffs. 'That's some spectacular scenery over there. All it needs is a little developmental work. I could——'

'No, Robert—please.' She put her hand on his arm, and he brought the jeep to a halt in the middle of the road. Not that that made any difference; there were hardly twenty vehicles on the whole island.

'Please what?' He sounded absentminded, as if his thoughts were on a different plane, far away.

'Please don't make Saba a project,' she begged. 'We— really like it the way it is.'

'It could be better, Laura.'

'Maybe—but don't *you* do it, Robert. I couldn't bear it if you were the one to tear everything up and re-do it. I just couldn't bear that.' She shivered and huddled down in the seat, her eyes straight forward to avoid looking at him. The silence lasted for a dozen years.

I've really given myself away, she thought angrily. Anger at herself, not him. It was a wonderful feeling when kept to herself. This—what name can I put on it? Friendship? Not enough! Love? Perhaps a shade too much, but somewhere in between those two words are the emotions I feel towards him. A rising tide, carrying all my defences before it, scattering all my principles, locking my strict upbringing behind solid closed doors. What would Gramps say about this? Or Anne? Instantly, her sister's laughing face appeared in her mind. Anne—always laughing, always beautiful, always an anchor for her little sister. A tear managed to squeeze itself out of her left eye. Rob caught it with a finger just as it rolled to the middle of her cheek.

'Hey, don't take it all *that* seriously!' his muted baritone coaxed. Laura sniffed back a pair of other tears and gave him a weak smile.

'I don't,' she said softly. He stared at her for a moment longer. What does he think I'm taking seriously? she asked herself in a flash of inspiration. The real-estate development or the love?

'C'mon,' prodded Emerald from the seat behind them. 'We can't sit here all day. There's another car coming.'

'Where?' Rob challenged doubtfully.

'Down there.' She pointed along the road to Bottom where, a full half-mile away, another jeep was slowly making its way up to the crest.

'I hate traffic jams,' he muttered, and shifted into gear.

'Go carefully,' Laura warned. 'By the way, where's Stacey?'

'Oh, my God!' Rob whacked his forehand with one huge hand. 'I was going to pick her up—she wanted to see the sights. Do you mind?'

'No, not at all,' sighed Laura, knowing she would regret this day.

Stacey Mantoff was in no pleasant mood when they picked her up in front of the hotel. Without thinking, Laura moved to the back seat beside Emerald, leaving to the blonde woman the honour of sharing the front seat. 'I've been waiting for hours,' Stacey said icily.

Rob looked casually at his watch. 'One, I'll grant you. We were sidetracked.'

'And you *had* to bring the children?'

'Luckily,' he returned. 'Laura brought the lunch for our picnic.'

'Picnic? Good Lord! I'd rather lunch at the hotel.'

'I could arrange that,' he said grimly. 'You could just stay here.'

Stacey shifted gears quickly. 'No—no, of course I want to go with you.' She leaned over and kissed his cheek. 'Go ahead, darling.' Emerald started to say something, but Laura squeezed the girl's hand and shook her head.

Robert started the car. 'I could use some directions,' he called back to Laura.

'Turn left here at the crossroads.'

He remembered the crossroads. One turned right and went down into the crater towards Bottom. And if one turned left—he jammed on the brakes. The road led straight to the edge of the cliffs. 'Hey, wait just a darn minute!' he exclaimed.

Laura giggled, and Emerald laughed outright. 'Fort Bay is straight down there,' the little girl instructed. 'Straight down.'

'Not exactly straight,' her mother admonished. 'More likely very crooked. Go ahead.'

Rob shifted into first gear. They bumped a couple of times on purposeful obstructions in the road. A sign appeared. 'Steep Descent,' it said in big red letters. 'Travel in second gear. Test brakes before descending. Up-bound traffic has right of way.'

'Yeah, sure,' he sighed. 'How far down?'

'To the water's edge,' Laura said solemnly. 'Not more than a thousand feet, I should think.' He took a deep breath and eased off on the brakes.

# CHAPTER SIX

'I THOUGHT we'd have our lunch on the beach,' said Rob. Laura strangled a giggle. He sounded so disappointed, so surprised.

'There isn't any beach, not anywhere on the island,' Emerald chimed in. 'This is it. This is all there is!'

*This* was a stretch about two hundred yards long, where a relatively flat section some twenty yards wide came gently down to the sea. But there was no sand. Everything was rock—huge granite chunks or multitudes of pumice pebbles, the leftovers of the vaguely distant eruption. On the landward side a platform had been built—of volcanic rock, naturally—and on top of this stood the tiny Customs House and an adjacent warehouse.

'I don't think much of *this*,' grumbled Stacey. They ignored her comment.

'Two flags?' asked Rob.

'Of course. Saba is a member of the Dutch Antilles, six little islands. Together they're an autonomous part of the Kingdom of the Netherlands. We share a queen, and a few monetary policies, but that's all.'

'Pardon my ignorance.' He didn't look a bit crestfallen. Emerald likes that, Laura thought. So do I! Almost at their feet, a heavily loaded rowing-boat had swung sideways in the surf as eight local men struggled to bring it closer to shore. The men on the near side of the craft were up to their ankles in water. Those on the far side were up to their chests. Offshore, an old freighter stood by, still with steam up. A little farther out, a slim cruise ship was doing the same.

'This is the harbour?' Stacey asked in astonishment.

'You bet,' Emerald confirmed. 'Everything that comes by boat comes here. Some little bitty stuff comes on the airplane, but not much. That regular airplane can carry only seven passengers.'

'Then why don't the ships anchor out there?'

'Out there?' Laura grinned at Stacey. 'Do you see that red buoy? That marks the edge of the island shelf. It's only fifty feet out from here. Beyond that buoy the depth drops off to fifty fathoms. Out where those ships are and that's about as close as they can safely come—it's about a hundred fathoms to solid bottom, and ships just can't carry that much anchor line. Are you importing something, Mr Carlton?'

'Something like that.' Rob wasn't about to expand on the answer, and she was too nervous to ask. Nervous? Why nervous? Just because he's standing there so closely? Come on, girl!

'Why don't you see to your business and we'll find a place to set out the lunch?' she suggested. He considered the question for a moment, then nodded and walked off.

'Where?' Stacey prompted glumly. 'Lunch, I mean.'

'At the base of the old pier. There really isn't anyplace else that's both dry and clean, is there?' Laura led the way, picking her trail carefully, carrying the basket. Emerald, moving slowly behind her on the rugged terrain, concentrated on where she put her steps. Laura checked out of the corners of her eyes, but said nothing. Confidence was the biggest thing the child needed. Confidence in herself and in her loved ones. Stacey struggled along behind, tottering on her high heels and glaring at the world.

The pier was a small stone construction, reaching out twenty-five feet or more, where the occasional passenger might land. Most opted for the second choice—to come in aboard the small boats, just as the freight was doing, and then be snatched up and carried, one at a time, up to the dry ground.

Laura opened the picnic basket and spread the table-cloth packed on top over the solid stone. And they waited. And waited. It took more than an hour for Rob to finish his business; when he came down to them, Emerald had not been able to wait. She had devoured her share of fried chicken, had had more than her share of the pound cake, and had gone off to watch the workmen.

'Don't get any ideas above your station, Doctor,' Stacey hissed at her the moment they were alone. 'He belongs to me!'

'Are you sure about that?' Laura returned. 'If so, you'd better watch out. He likes to wander off the reservation!'

Rob's appearance closed the brief debate. He sat down beside Laura, perhaps a little too close for comfort. She shifted half an inch or so, then decided it was pure cowardice and moved back again. 'Breezy cold for a tropical beach,' he observed.

'I hadn't noticed any cold.'

'We'd be a lot warmer if I——' and his arm came around her shoulders and pulled her against him. It certainly was cold, wasn't it? her conscience gibed at her. Oh, shut up! she muttered as she squirmed a little closer and rested her head on his shoulder, uninvited. It *was* more comfortable, but it was only a taste, and she wanted more. Not here. But somewhere, soon, she promised herself. Twenty-eight years is too long to wait! I want everything!

'Good heavens, she can't be that cold!' Stacey interrupted. Her voice loses its polish when she's angry, Laura thought.

'I'd rather not fight,' Rob said smoothly. 'I'm an equal opportunity employer.' He waved his other arm and Stacey joined them in an uneasy threesome.

It isn't just that he's an available man, Laura reasoned. It's because he's—my Robert. I don't want *any* man, I want *him*. I want him so badly that I can *taste* it! But I don't intend to share him—not with someone like Stacey!

'Did you say something?' His lips were at her ear, as if he were a little hungry himself. Startled, she moved away from him.

'I said let's have some chicken. You must be hungry!' trying to keep the little quaver out of her voice.

'Yes, I'm very hungry.' And how can he make those few words sound like a sensual invitation? she thought, bewildered by everything that was happening inside herself.

Rob juggled the chicken, reluctant to take his arm from around her. He stared at her ear, as if he meant to begin his meal there. And then, almost as if he had put the whole idea aside, he shifted a little and began to gnaw on the chicken leg.

Laura and Stacey were standing by the jeep when Emerald came back. Rob had gone back into the Customs House for one last check on his papers. The little girl was a small package of excitement, but obviously tired. She was favouring her injured leg more than usual, but smiled all the same. She crept around the back of the jeep to surprise her mother with a hug.

'Do you like that man, Mama?'

It was a clear-blue-sky question, and Laura hardly knew how to field it. 'Robert, you mean?'

'Of course, Robert. We don't have any other man around, do we?'

'Well, there's always Mr Van Hooten up on the hill.'

'Oh, Mama! Mr Van Hooten is around, but he's not around us. Mr Carlton is around us! Do you like him?'

'I should think a child that age should have learned more manners,' Stacey said haughtily.

'Argue with me all you want,' Laura said softly, 'but don't you dare sharpen your tongue on my daughter, lady. We don't have a lot of time for sophistication. Leave her alone or I'll bash you one!'

'Barbarian!' the other woman muttered.

'And don't you forget it,' Laura added fiercely.

'Well, I like him a lot,' Emerald interjected. 'An awful lot!'

'I'm glad to hear that!' Rob was standing behind the little girl, out of her line of vision. He leaned down over Emerald's head. 'It *was* me you were talking about, wasn't it?'

'Of course it was,' the little girl sparkled. 'We both like you. Only——'

'Only what?'

'Only Belle—I'm not sure about Belle. She said something about schemers and conniv—I can't remember—it was a big word.'

'And was that all?' he teased.

'Emerald!' Laura commanded. But there was no stopping the little minx.

'She said you'd better watch your step, 'cause if you didn't she was going to put crawlers in your soup and sand in your socks!' The little girl stopped to consider the two astonished adult faces. 'I wouldn't like to have sand in my socks. It feels terrible.'

'Yes, well——' Rob was struggling to control his voice, to keep it solemn, but was not having a great deal of success. 'I'm not sure having crawlers in my soup is all that much better. Believe me, I'll be careful.'

'You could kiss her,' Emerald suggested.

'Who? Belle?'

'No—that's stupid. You could kiss my mama.'

'No, he couldn't,' exclaimed Laura, climbing into the seat. Her face was overheated. The noonday sun, she told herself—but it was a long time after noon already.

'I don't think your mother agrees,' sighed Rob. 'How about you, Emerald?'

'Oh, I don't mind,' the child replied. She climbed up into the jeep to get a height advantage, then wrapped both her thin arms around his neck and kissed him, once on each cheek.

'Could we perhaps get back home?' Stacey was not enjoying life. She was battered by the wind, tired from the climbing, and annoyed by the specious conversation.

Emerald giggled as she climbed in and sat on Laura's lap. The ride home was quick and sure. Rob and Emerald talked all the way, joking, teasing, daring each other to do a million things or more. Laura was quiet, half listening, evaluating all the things about herself that she had learned in that one short day. She wanted to believe them all. She wanted him to be *my Robert*. And yet she felt a little fearful. It was if she were standing in the door of a plane, waiting to make her first parachute jump. She wanted to go with all her might, but her craven heart cautioned otherwise.

It was a disappointment when Rob dropped them off at the house. 'I have to take Stacey back to Windwardside, and there's some work to be done there,' he explained.

'I suppose I have to do my exercises,' grumbled Emerald.

'No, I don't think so, dear. You've done enough exercising for one day. Belle isn't back yet—she wanted to go visit in the village. Why don't we just go around and relax by the pool, both of us?'

'I'd like that, Mama.'

Laura put an arm around the girl, feeling her tremble. 'Does it hurt, love?'

'No. It's just—tired, I guess. It doesn't hurt.'

They helped each other around the house. Laura pulled open a couple of the folded aluminium lounge chairs and they sank into them.

'That was nice, that trip. I like to be with Mr Carlton. I really do.'

'I do too, dear.' But he doesn't belong to me, Laura thought bitterly. Stacey owns him! The two Lackland women sat wrapped in their separate dreams until Belle came home.

The elderly woman sank into a chair beside them and the air *whoofed* out of her. 'I went all the way up them stairs,' she sighed. 'All the way. You remember Mrs Vanderhoof, Missy? She send her best regards, and say the tooth you fix is good as new. Where that man is?'

'He had some more business to tend to,' Emerald reported.

More likely that he had to soothe Princess Stacey, Laura thought gloomily. Belle studied Laura's face. 'What you need, Missy——' she started to say, when a noise from the house interrupted. 'What was that?'

The three of them looked at each other. 'A bell ringing?'

'In the house, Mama. I'll go see.'

'All right, love. And bring out your lotion when you come, I'll do your leg massage before it gets too dark.'

The child was gone for about ten minutes, during which time Belle and Laura exchanged gossip of old friends and old places. 'I gonna hate to leave this island, Missy. But I suppose we have to go?' queried Belle.

'Of course we must,' Laura said. 'Emerald will be twelve in a couple of months. It's time she went to a better school and saw more of the world. It's time she began to realise, too, what it means to be one of the richest little girls in the world. I have a scheme planned, but I'm not sure where. We have Grandpa Lackland's house in Hartford available, and Grandpa Jacob's house on Long Island. Or we could rent or buy something just for ourselves. How about that, Belle? Emerald will be off with some man by the time she's twenty—eight years. Maybe this would be a good time for you and me to find a small town where I could set up a practice and we could settle down after Emerald leaves us?'

'Nonsense, Missy! Time we got *you* settled down. Time we found you a man of your own. Then we don't gotta worry about when Emerald leaves us.'

'Oh, Belle, please! You know that's not likely to happen. I'm almost thirty. Men—even older men—are looking for the young ones these days.'

'How about this here Mr Carlton?'

'I—he's nice, Belle. But he's only here on a holiday, with a woman from his own society. When it's over, do you think he'll even remember my name? Time to face it, dear: men don't think of dentists when they're in a romantic mood. When was the last time you ever read a story that had a dentist for a heroine?'

'I disremembers, Missy,' Belle maintained stoutly, 'but that got nothin' to do with you. You a beautiful woman, with lots of talents. An' I don't mean just with teeth or paintbrushes, neither!'

'Mama?' Emerald walked slowly out of the house, trying to hide a smile.

'What is it, love?'

'Do you know what happened while we were away today?'

'No, obviously I don't,' chuckled Laura. 'But you're about to tell us?'

'Yes. Somebody put in a telephone in the house!'

'Well, I never!' muttered Belle.

'I *told* him he'd have to wait for months for an installation.' Laura shook her head slowly. 'Which only goes to prove, never dare a tycoon. Imagine that? It's only been a week or two, and it's already in!'

'That man a fast one, Missy. You just watch your step, you hear? He gets a telephone in no time? How long it gonna take before he gets what else he wants?'

'What *are* you talking about, Belle?'

'You don't know? How come you face so red?'

'Belle—I——' protested Laura.

'Well, doesn't anyone want to know what the call was about?' Emerald moved in between them and settled on the concrete apron of the pool.

'The call? Oh lord, I'd forgotten. Where is the telephone, and who called?'

'It's in his bedroom, Mama, sitting right by his bed. And it was Miss Mantoff that called. Said Mr Carlton was still at work, and would stay at the hotel and have supper with her. She sounded very pleased with herself.'

'I suppose she has reason to be,' Laura replied. 'Now, let me have that lotion, and you stretch out here on the lounger while I do the massage. And Belle can be getting our supper. Perhaps something simple—say, a mushroom omelette?'

'I hears you,' the old lady said. 'Nice young woman, that one? Old enough to be crow-bait. And you, you don't care a bit, does you, Missy!'

'Belle! There are little ears present!'

'You can tell me tomorrow, Belle,' the little ears called after her. 'And you don't have to be so rough, Mama. You're supposed to *massage* my leg, not break it off!'

No matter how she tried, Laura could not sleep that night. The other two had long since gone off to Nod, and she was prowling the living-room. The meal had been excellent, and she couldn't eat another bite. There was work to be done in her studio, but she had long since committed herself never to use a brush under artificial light. There was work to be done in the dental office too, but her fingers fumbled as she tried to pick up the tools, so she quickly gave that up. A long shower helped to pass some of the time, but not enough. When she finally heard the roar of the engine, she jumped up and hurried to the door, paying no attention to the fact that her robe was loosely tied.

'I didn't expect this,' Rob told her as he strode in and gathered her up in his arms.

'I didn't either,' she said. 'I just couldn't——'

'Couldn't help yourself?'

'I—I'm afraid that's so, Robert. I—I think I must be coming down with something.'

'It's going around,' he chuckled. 'I think I've been bitten by the same bug.'

'You? How could that be?'

'When did you last look in a mirror, young lady?'

'Oh—about ten minutes ago.' Laura was trying to act casual about the whole affair, when she felt anything but! The warmth of him, the strength, the smell of maleness, all were working on her sensitivities—had worked. They had breached a gap ten miles wide in her defences, and she held her breath, wondering if he were about to continue the assault. He stood for a moment, thinking, then he slipped one arm under her knees and carried her down the corridor to her own bedroom.

She had left a small lamp lit on the bedside table. Rob put her down on her feet in front of the full-length wall mirror, and turned the lamp up as high as it would go. Her hair was loose, surrounding her face with its halo of golden curls. The door was closed. Laura shivered in anticipation.

He came back behind her, circling her waist with his arms. 'You're a beautiful woman, Laura. Stop running yourself down. Look in the mirror.' His voice was part of the total effect; she stood mesmerised as he slowly unfastened the tie of her robe and drew it off her shoulders, leaving her standing there without a stitch. 'Look in the mirror.' He knelt behind her, touching her feet and ankles. She followed him with her eyes, the trembling accentuating.

'Lovely feet,' he crooned softly as his hands massaged them gently. 'Strong, straight ankles. Legs—long, sexy, warm.' His hands went upward as he murmured, up the outside of her legs to the knee, back down, up the insides, moving gently up her inner thighs. Laura gasped at the suddenness of the shock as he touched her intimately, then moved up over the slight curve of her belly to the narrow span of her waist, then back down again, on the outside of her hips, cupping each curve. His words had escaped her. There was a buzzing in her ears and her internal controls had all disintegrated. The hands came back to her waist and travelled slowly up the incline of her breasts, pausing for a moment on their bronze tips.

By this time, Laura had given up breathing. It seemed unnecessary in the heat that swept up and down her spine. She rocked a little on her feet, and was forced to separate them to maintain her balance. Rob's hands pulled her back against his frame, and she could feel his arousal pushing madly at her. The hands circled. 'Such beautiful breasts,' he murmured in her ear. 'Each one a delight.'

She wanted to say that they were too small, but had trouble making any noise except a moan. Besides, surely he was a better judge than she was about such things? The hands moved away, up around her neck, up over her chin. A finger stopped in each dimple. It was *nice*, but did not feed the madness, the fire that he had ignited. She pulled both his hands down to her breasts again, and felt the explosion. She squirmed as one of his hands shifted down to rest gently on her mound of Venus. All her alarm bells went off. She struggled to recover, clutching at his wandering hands.

'What are you *doing* to me?' she whispered.

Rob laughed and gently kissed the nape of her neck. 'What are you *letting* me do to you?' he answered, and left her standing there. Moments later, the motor of the jeep roared outside the house, and went rattling up the hill.

'There you have it,' she muttered, still standing in front of the mirror. You're beautiful, Laura—but when he wants a *real* woman he gets back on his horse and goes looking for Stacey Mantoff.

But for the rest of that night she twisted and turned in her bed, trying to find an answer to his question. He was right, she had *let* him do it all. But why? The answer completely eluded her.

# CHAPTER SEVEN

'LOOK, I'm not sure what's going on,' Laura said stubbornly. It was Friday, the day they were to begin the tiresome trip to Puerto Rico for Emerald's last examination. And here was Belle throwing a monkey wrench into the process.

'What's goin' on is that *man*, he gonna help,' said Belle. Her round little jaw stuck out just as far as it could reach.

'You're a stubborn woman, Belle—yes, you are!'

'Not as much as I was,' the older woman returned. 'I give a whole pile of stubborn to you. He's gonna help. You too proud to be helped?'

'No, I'm *not* too proud——'

'Thank God for that!' Rob came around the corner of the house, hands in the pockets of his shorts, and a big grin on his face. 'After I heard all about going here and there and changing planes and taxis and lord knows what, I thought we might do things more easily. You really wouldn't want Emerald to arrive at the hospital already worn out, would you?'

'No,' Laura sighed. 'I hate that part of it. That's why we go a day early, so she can rest up. What have you got up your sleeve?'

'Me?' He peered at the short-sleeved sports shirt he was wearing. 'Nothing but kindness and love, Laura. Why are you so suspicious of me?'

'I wish I knew,' Laura muttered. 'I really wish I knew. *Emerald?*' she shouted back at the house.

'I'm coming!' The little girl came out of the house, not as spryly as usual, and with a paleness about her that bespoke fear. 'I don't really want to go,' she said.

'An' I don't know where *she* get her stubborn,' Belle said determinedly. 'You gotta go, honey.'

'Yes, you have to go,' Laura repeated, snuggling the girl up against her side. 'This is the last one, love. I'm sure it won't hurt the way the others did. And I'm sure you'll get your medical clearance. Just keep that in mind, young lady. This is what you've been aiming for over the past five years. And here it is—examination time.'

'Just like in school,' the girl muttered. 'I could flunk.'

'I don't see how, love. We've both worked hard. You've done all your exercises, and a great deal more swimming than required. Everything's going to be OK.'

The early morning sun caught the trembling smile on the little girl's face, just as a motor hummed, up on the highway, and turned into their drive. Not a rattletrap jeep, this, but an almost new sedan. Ari Van Hooten waved from the driver's seat.

'How about this, Miss Laura?' He leaned out of the window on the driver's side, the sun sparkling off his completely bald head.

'This is pretty fine,' she returned, walking the circumference of the vehicle, trailing a finger on its polished green paint. 'Do we get to ride, or just admire, Ari?'

'You get to ride,' he laughed. 'That man of yours rented it by the week. Tourists have all the money, don't they?'

Laura swung back and forth between answers. She wanted to deny that *he* was her man; at the same time, she wanted to disagree about the tourists. She wanted to ask him where Stacey might be but, contrarily, she didn't want to know. As a result, none of the words made it out into the open, and there was Robert, ushering her firmly into the front seat.

'And Belle, you and Emerald will sit in the back, right?'

'*All right!*' the pair of them chorused.

'Now wait just a darn minute!' protested Laura. Too late. Rob closed the back door behind the laughing pair, then joined her in the front seat. 'Give over, Laura, there's a good girl. Leave enough room for Mr Van Hooten to drive.'

'I can't give over any farther without ending up on the gear-stick,' she muttered. 'You did this on purpose!'

'Right,' he laughed in her ear, softly.

'Emerald could have been up here, and there would be plenty of room, and——'

'Right. Go ahead, Mr Van Hooten.'

'Adult women require a certain—larger amount of room to sit down in, and——'

'Right.'

'Stop saying *right* right in my ear! Stop rubbing my——'

'Hip, I think it's called. You are a well built lady, Doctor.'

Laura could feel the colour coming to her cheeks. Not that she was angry. To tell the truth, it was an offhand compliment, and she savoured it, even though she felt embarrassed. She pushed Rob's hand off her knee as she tried to pull her skirt down.

'What are you two whispering about up there?' Emerald demanded, leaning over the seat between them.

'We're talking about decorum,' snapped Laura.

'That's nice. What is it?'

'What kind of airplane is that down there?' Belle interrupted. 'Ain't got no wings. You ain't gonna get me flyin' in no airplane without wings!'

'It's a helicopter,' said Rob. He shifted in his seat so he could see the people in the back while talking to them. Naturally, it put him off balance, and he put a hand back on Laura's knee to steady himself.

There's certainly nothing wrong with that, she told herself. He *has* to hang on to something, and there's not much else available, is there? Besides, he's already seen more of me than any man in the world, so why should I worry if he wants to play 'kneesies'? What else could happen, with Emerald and Belle here? Practising? Trying to keep his hand in until he gets back to the big city? So what do I do, brainy girl? Push him away, tell him off, or make believe that nothing's going on? That last choice, but if he moves that hand any farther——

But the choice did not come up again. They came off the last zag in the hand-laid rock road, and scooted out on to the tarmac of the tiny airport on the Vlakke Hoek. The helicopter was more modern than the last one in which Rob had ridden; it was equipped for air and sea rescue, with a two-man paramedic crew. They were welcomed cheerfully in a mixture of Dutch and French, and strapped into their seats. Emerald sat up close to her window, enthralled by everything she saw. But Laura was not a happy traveller; her favourite mode of transport was walking. This clumsy craft, with its rotors circling just overhead, looked like a pregnant June bug that could hardly get them off the ground. She wanted to tell somebody that, but the noise-level was too high. Robert, sitting beside her, touched her hand lightly. She felt immeasurably improved.

One of the crew members came round with headsets for everyone, equipment which allowed them to use the amplifier system in the craft. Rob slipped a pair over Laura's head, and laughed to see Emerald, refusing help, struggling to do it herself.

'How's that, can you hear?' he asked Laura, and she smiled up at him and squeezed his hand. He talked to her about nothing at all while the engine reverberated and the craft shook. Soothing talk, of no importance, just comforting noises that lulled her to sleep as the helicopter vaulted into the air. She was still asleep when they landed at Frederiksted on the island of Ste Croix, for refuelling, and barely struggled to awareness when the aircraft settled on to the emergency pad just outside the University Hospital in Puerto Rico. Before she could get both eyes open, Emerald was being shepherded away by a nurse, after chattering with Rob at ten words to the second.

'Robert!' He came over to her immediately and put an arm around her shoulders.

'She'll be all right, Laura. She's caught on to the excitement of it, and wants to go it alone.'

'But she's only eleven. Dear lord, she's just a baby!'

'Not that, Laura. Come on now—wipe your eyes, perk up, and we'll go in to see her settled.'

'And then I suppose you've got something else planned?' She was no longer angry with his meddling—in fact, she was enjoying it. Her wristwatch showed her that they had taken only three hours on the direct flight of barely a hundred miles. It would have taken them the whole day, with numberless changes and waits and delays, had the three women come by themselves. More than that, her independent spirit admitted, it was *nice* to have a man around to handle all the little details.

'If I tell you, you promise not to yell at me?' They sauntered up the wide walk that led to the admissions section, hand in hand, Belle panting behind them.

'No, I won't yell,' Laura promised.

'In that case, I have reservations for us at the Condado Beach Hotel,' Rob told her. 'I'm assured that, with such an early start, Emerald will be ready to leave for home just after noon tomorrow. The helicopter will be here waiting for us at that time. And, in the meantime, we three can see how the richer half lives.'

'Gambling casinos?'

'You don't approve? Then how about a walk through Old San Juan, and a tour of El Morro, one of the oldest castles in the New World? We'll throw caution to the wind, and live it up!'

'I ain't much for throwin' to the wind,' Belle commented. 'But you and Missy can. I jus' like to go barefoot and walk in the sand and touch the ocean.'

'You miss your island, Belle?'

'Not really, Missy. Well, maybe I do. But I was very young when my mama take us all Stateside. What I remember is jus' the sound of the sea, and the soft of the sand between the toes. Maybe some day, when you get— when things settle down, I take a vacation an' go back to Haiti, me.'

They made it back to the hospital on time. The helicopter sat quietly on its pad, Emerald was hovering anxiously at the admissions desk, and Laura's feet were worn to the ankles. Her daughter was wearing a brilliant new dress, Laura noted, one that *she* had never seen before. And she was carrying two more in those long plastic covers one sees when clothes come back from the cleaners. But the situation was too exciting, too emotion-packed, to leave room for enquiry.

The doctor joined them a few minutes later.

'Dr Lackland!' He loved to use her title. It established a kinship, and a man on the wrong side of sixty likes to feel an occasional closeness to a beautiful woman on the right side of thirty. 'Well, I can see that you and Emerald have been working out religiously. Everything is A-OK. The musculation is just what we wanted. The bone graft is perfect. We can turn our little lady loose and see how she runs.'

'She'll be tired, though, doctor?'

'For the first while. Just keep an eye on her to be sure she doesn't overdo it. Don't be alarmed if there's some small pain now and then. Use the pills I gave you before. There are still a great many adjustments that little frame has to make—but I'm sure she'll make them. And don't hesitate to contact me again, if you feel it necessary.'

'I won't, Doctor.' Her artist's hand was enveloped in his surgeon's paw, and he was pumping away. 'But my contract runs out in two months, and then we'll be going back Stateside. I might want a referral when we decide where to settle.'

'Just drop me a line,' he offered. 'And now kindly get this little imp out of here. She talks up a storm, and my hospital is in an uproar!' He was a tall thin man, slightly balding, and when he leaned over to kiss Emerald his glasses fell off his nose. Before they hit the ground Rob had rescued them. 'Great fielding!' the doctor smiled. 'The only ones I have left. I manage to break three or four pairs a month.'

'Strictly luck,' Rob returned. 'Come on, ladies. I feel like a shepherd dog running the flock back to the corral!'

Rested, refreshed, happy, Laura stayed awake on the return trip. The other two dropped off to sleep as soon as they were airborne.

'Huh, lucky,' she said softly. 'I suppose you played professional ball?'

He grinned down at her, and his voice sounded a little metallic through the amplifier system. 'Nope. Never good enough, lady. Great catch, no hit, that's what they told me. Does that put you off me? Are you a sports buff?'

'Only with the Red Sox,' she laughed. 'I used to cut classes—I went to Tufts, in Boston, you know. On bright sunny days, I would have a terrible sickness that could only be cured by going out to Fenway Park to watch the Sox play.'

'And you never got caught at it?' He shook his head as if surprised.

'Only once,' she laughed. 'I sneaked off from m afternoon class, and got a seat in the grandstand, right next to the professor who was supposed to be teaching the class! We agreed not to squeal on each other.'

It was fun, talking to him, relaxed. The headsets shut out some of the engine noises, and Rob's arm around her shoulders was very proprietorial, and very—appreciated. I wonder what he's thinking? Laura asked herself.

I wonder what she's thinking? Rob asked himself. What a complete damn fool I was the other night! What difference does it make if she has a child and doesn't want to admit the sexual connotations? What difference does it make if she's out to trap me—into marriage? Because that's just exactly what I want to trap *her* into. Maybe, if we both scheme enough, we'll both succeed. Forget about her past. Your own can't stand a great deal of looking at either, buddy. You have to learn to trust her. That's the happy word from this time on. Trust her. God, I hope she doesn't blow her stack when she gets home and sees the rest of this caper!

Laura tugged at his arm. 'You really love all this, don't you?' she said.

'All this what?'

'All this being able to arrange for helicopters and schedule changes, and being in charge of everything and everybody?'

Yes, I love it, he thought. And her. I love the power of being able to summon up the flying carpet with just a snap of the fingers. It isn't the money that I need, it's the power. And if I give her one tiny hint of what's on my mind, she'll run like a scared rabbit!

'Does that bother you?' he asked.

She sighed and rested her head on his shoulder. 'I thought it would,' she admitted. 'But now—I'm surprised to find I don't. It's all—rather nice—the companionship, the sharing, the laughter. I don't——'

She paused for too long; Rob gave her a verbal prod. 'You don't what?'

Laura laughed—at herself, he knew—and the words tumbled out. 'I don't find it as difficult to get along with a man as I've always thought!'

'I'm glad to hear that,' he chuckled. 'Why is Belle smiling? I thought she was asleep.'

'I is,' the old lady commented, opening one eye. 'Fast asleep. Go ahead talkin'. I don't mind to hear the dove birds in the trees.' Her eye closed, but the smile remained.

'Chaperon,' he groused amiably. 'Just can't get away from them, can we? Look at that!'

Down below them, etched like paintings in a painted sea, a pair of tall ships raced each other, their masts crowded with sail.

'It doesn't seem that we're moving,' whispered Laura. 'It looks as if we're standing still and the world's moving below us. Oh, Robert, I'm so happy!' The blush again, unsummoned, undesired. 'Because Emerald is well again,' she hurried on. 'Because she can run and jump and be a normal kid from now on.' A pause to reflect. 'And it's nice that you're here too.'

'Thanks a whole lot,' he said dolefully. 'Lucky we don't have a cat.'

'What?'

'I said, it's lucky we don't have a cat. When I was young we had three cats, and I always felt that, as the family went, I rated well below the cats.'

'Well, if we had a cat, you'd rate higher,' she said whimsically. 'Not too much higher, but some!'

'I've always liked compliments,' he returned with injured dignity.

Laura took the curse off the words by loosening her safety-belt far enough so that she could kiss his warm, rough cheek. 'I'll bet you have to shave twice a day, Robert.'

'It depends entirely on what I'm doing and who I'm doing it with.' Rob shifted his arm away, and she protested with a tiny moan.

'Hold me,' she whispered. 'I need you to hold me.'

'It will be my pleasure,' he returned, 'just as soon as I can wake up the muscles in my arm.'

She abandoned her seat-belt entirely, leaned over against him, and tucked the top of her head under his chin. It was a nice fit. The motors droned on, the blades whipped at the air, the sun glistened on the blue Caribbean waters, and everything in Laura's world was at peace.

It was cool by the pool—cool and restful. Laura checked her watch. Four hours ago they had been in Puerto Rico, in the centre of urban bustle. And Mr Fixit was standing over her now, as she relaxed in her lounger.

'I sent Emerald in for a nap, Robert. I think it's time you and I had another little talk.' She patted the edge of the lounge chair, and he lowered himself down. Having him sitting down made things less traumatic.

'I think a *big* talk is indicated. Ladies first.' Laura's ear was still slightly blocked from the flight; at least, she thought that was the problem. Otherwise why would he sound so—nervous? She tucked in her stubborn little chin and had at it.

'It would seem that you were playing Father Christmas while we were in Puerto Rico. Was that necessary?'

'Necessary? Does it have to be a necessity for me to want to buy a beautiful little girl a couple of dresses and things?'

'"And things" is right! Everything but a diamond tiara. How did that escape your notice?'

He chuckled. 'I thought that might be just the slightest bit ostentatious.' He was doing his best to walk over the fire-pit of her anger on a rope of humour, and from the look on Laura's face he was having no luck at all. It was hard to look innocent under her penetrating stare. Perhaps he should go on the offensive.

'You talk as if I have no right to spend my own money on someone whom I like very much,' Rob argued. 'That's all it was, an expression of—love!'

Lau. struggled to sit up straighter. A more suspicious person could hardly be found, her expression said. 'And that's all it was? Robert—are you engaged in some sort of underground warfare to steal my daughter away from me?'

'Me?' Injured innocence, that had to be the only way out for him. 'Now, why would I want to do that?'

'To get at me,' she returned bluntly. 'To come between Emerald and me somehow. To try to force us to make a decision in your favour. To make——'

'Missy! Miss Laura! Glory be!' Belle burst out of the kitchen, waving both hands. Out of the corner of her eye, Laura saw Robert duck his head, almost like a turtle withdrawing to safety.

'Belle, calm down. What is it?'

'You don't see what is it? You don't look in the kitchen, and in the living-room, and—and everywheres?'

'Of course I didn't,' Laura said quietly. 'You know I came directly out here to get a breath of air. No, that's not true: I *did* stop in the bathroom. Something *did* look strange. What?'

'Electric, that's what,' laughed Belle. 'What a wonderful thing you do, Miss Laura. To surprise me, hey? Me, I am plenty surprised. I am pretty tired from oil lamps—and now I got electric!'

'*Robert!*' He had risen and was doing his best to move casually out of reach. When her firm voice snapped his name he was caught with one foot still in the air, like a performer on a high-wire. He set the other foot down carefully. 'Yes?'

'What about it?'

'What about what, Laura?'

'Who electrified my house in just two days?'

'Oh, that! It makes a problem?'

'Of course it's a problem! There aren't any wires coming out this far, and I wasn't about to install a gasoline generator. And besides, the rates on this island are astronomical. Just what have you been up to?'

'It's only a small change, Laura. You said I might make any small changes I thought necessary.'

'Yes?' There was not enough warmth in the one word to keep a cup of tea at the Equator.

'And I found it impossible to do so without my computer.'

'You mean to tell me you brought one of those huge computers into *my* house?'

'Not exactly. In fact, it's a very small computer. It comes in a briefcase, and fits on the top of the desk in my bedroom. But of course, it needs a modest amount of electricity. So, since there was a lot left over, I thought of Belle in her kitchen, and Emerald for her homework. And even you for your dental office!' And if I could figure out a way to get Motherhood and Apple Pie in there, I would have said that too, he told himself. Maybe I should have included God and His church? And yet she doesn't sound *boiling* mad—just a little displeased? Look at you, Rob Carlton. You're actually shaking! Standing to judgement in front of this tiny little thing. Lo, how are the mighty fallen!

'So what did you do?' asked Laura. 'Buy the power company?'

'No, not at all. The thought never crossed my mind. I had considered a generator, but I supposed it might clash with your art work, what with the noise and all——'

'Robert, you're fumbling for words! Come to the point. Where does the electricity come from, and how in the world do you think I can afford some monstrous electricity bill?'

'It's all free. It comes through the air,' he laughed, pointing to the mountainside just above them. Barely visible above the tops of the palm trees Laura saw the revolving blades—of a windmill. 'If there's one thing you have constantly on this island,' Rob commented, 'it's wind. So there was this electric generator powered by a wind machine available at Sint Maarten—for a song, so to speak. I snapped it up, had it shipped over, and there it is. It doesn't disturb the scenery, requires very little maintenance, and doesn't make a sound. Certainly, it meets all your criteria.' He looked too solemn to be true, this big, handsome man trying to appeal to Caesar. If it were possible, thought Laura, he looks like a little boy, hat in hand. But he's not, is he? He's a power in the world we live in. I mustn't misjudge. But it was hard for her to be sober and dignified in such a situation.

'Darn you, Rob Carlton,' she laughed, 'you sound like a dealer in second-hand camels!'

'What a terrible thing to say, Missy!' Belle interrupted.

'Took the words right out of my mouth,' added Rob. The pair of them stood there watching her, shaking their heads. And it's all a put-on! Laura thought.

'Darn it! Look at the both of you. Conspirators! Butter wouldn't melt in your mouths! I——' But my argument isn't with Belle, she remembered, it's with this—man! 'Thank you, Belle. Are you going to make us some lunch?'

Belle cocked her head to one side, nodded, and went back to her kitchen, humming a little song.

'Now,' said Laura, 'we'll get back to the discussion.' She swung both her legs up on to the lounger and re-arranged her skirt.

'Is that what it is?' asked Rob, challenging. 'I thought it was an inquisition. Is the guilty rascal allowed to sit?' She moved her feet aside and he joined her. The slender construction of tubes and canvas creaked dangerously.

'Do be careful,' she warned. And you be careful too, Laura Lackland, she lectured herself. The minute he starts to get close is the time when you lose control of the game. Look at those eyes! You could drown yourself entirely in them. And that stupid hank of hair that keeps falling down over his forehead. Heavenly days, there's a grey streak in it! Her hand went to him and pushed the errant lock back.

'You're getting prematurely grey,' she murmured as her fingers lingered over the task.

'I didn't do it all by myself,' Rob returned softly. 'I've had a great deal of help lately.' Before she could recover her hand he had it imprisoned, and raised it to his lips. The kiss fell on her open palm, and a shudder ran up and down her spine. An emotion she had confined for years was snarling to be released from its cage. Laura summoned up strength and stamped down the rebellion.

'So it wasn't just clothes for Emerald—which I appreciate, by the way. Setting aside the idea that I would prefer to buy things myself for my daughter, I'm well aware how much time and energy it takes, shopping for a child her age. So I *do* approve, and appreciate your thoughtfulness.'

'Thank God for that,' he rumbled. And the last thing in the world I'm going to tell her right this minute is that I hired the shopping service at the hotel to do the work. But I deserve the credit. After all, it *was* my idea.

'But I—well, you make even the electricity sound plausible, and that's what makes me suspicious. Isn't there an old Arab story about the camel who got his nose in the tent one cold night, and ended up dispossessing the owner?'

'I was never much for old Arabs,' Rob said solemnly. 'And I have no intention of dispossessing you.' Not at all, honest Injun, he thought. What I'm after now, little lady, is *possessing* you and all you possess. New goal—an early New Year resolution. Rob Carlton is to put away all his doubts and suspicions, and marry this girl!

'Laura?' He had come across those inches that separated them, and his cheek was warm against her own. Before she heard the question her face turned towards him, and her lips snatched at happiness. There was warmth and love and passion—and something else—in that kiss. Something more than a contact between human beings. Something indefinable and sweet.

'What are you two doing?'

The voice was right in Laura's ear, a lilting, laughing question whose answer was already known. It startled both the adults. Rob sat up in a hurry, the fragile aluminium rod of the lounger snapped and the entire contraption turned on its side. And since it had been sitting only inches from the coping of the pool, it dumped its load of people into the water!

Laura came up spluttering and laughing at the same time. A moment later there was an eruption beside her, somewhat like the bow wave that a Wright whale speeds ahead of it as it comes up for air, and Rob was beside her, treading water. 'Are you all right?' he gasped.

'I'm OK,' she gurgled, 'but you look a sight!'

'So, I'm not beautiful,' he growled menacingly, and pushed her under.

'Hey, you leave my mother alone!' Indignant words in a high, sweet voice reached them. A smaller splash, and Emerald was beside them, gliding in that natural stroke with which islanders are born.

'He's not hurting me, love,' laughed Laura. 'And I thought I told you to take a nap?'

'I did,' the child reported. Both adults reached for her head, and pushed her under. She came up giggling at the other side of the pool.

I needed all that, Laura thought. And, besides, it puts an end to any more embarrassment. She brushed her long hair out of her eyes and defied Rob with a look. Dared him to do—something. Seconds later, she wished she hadn't. Robert Carlton was not the man to pass up a dare.

He snatched her up close, held her secure against her half-hearted struggles to be free, and allowed them both to sink slowly to the bottom of the pool, wrapped in another kiss. It was not the first time Laura had been kissed underwater. But the other occasions were long ago and far away, as far back as her high-school days, with boys who were just learning the difference between men and women. The thought of those days of pre-history disturbed her. She kicked gently, broke loose, and came back up before Rob did. Emerald was dog-paddling in front of her.

'What I came out to tell you is that Belle says lunch is ready, and you'd better hustle, Mama. Your dress is soaking!'

'So is yours, love. What did I warn you about? Men are nothing but trouble!'

'But you kind of liked that trouble, didn't you?'

'Impudent child! Sort of——' Laura corrected, fumbling for words. 'Not "kind of". We say "sort of".'

'I think we're all kind of drowning out here,' chuckled Rob, coming up for air behind them. Emerald looked at her mother with that tinge of childish amusement that arises when two adults disagree.

'Remember, I'm your mother,' Laura threatened as she struck out for the side of the pool. 'What does *he* know?'

They were all at the lunch table half an hour later, dried and dressed. It was still early in the afternoon, but Belle had turned on the electric light—not surprisingly, a lamp in the shape of a candle. Emerald could not resist playing with it. As a result, they ate with lights alternately flashing at them.

'It's been a wonderful day,' Laura announced when the plates were empty. The adults had white wine in front of them; Emerald's glass held lemonade. 'I propose a toast.' She raised her glass first in the child's direction. 'To Emerald, who passed her exam with flying colours.' They all touched glasses and sipped.

'And now to the House of Carlton,' she proposed, 'which has done miracles this weekend in aid of the peasants.'

Rob touched his glass to hers, his eyes gleaming at her over the tops of them. Under his breath, audible only to Laura, he added, 'And to all those who will join that House.'

The thought and the words followed Laura to bed that night, bringing in their wake some very explicit and erotic dreams.

## CHAPTER EIGHT

LAURA was busy in her office on the following Saturday. It had been a very busy work week, and she was worried. The girl in Chair One had a bad case of gingivitis, and Laura worked carefully. To a twelve-year-old, a smile was of extreme importance. The treatment was not complicated: scrape away all the plaque and tartar which had trapped bacteria on the teeth, coat everything in sight with fluoride, and prescribe a course of penicillin to reduce the gum infection. And then, in as awesome a tone as she could find, add a long lecture about snacks and sweets and daily brushing with a good toothpaste. When the girl escaped, happy to be out from under the gun, Laura turned around, and almost knocked over her tray of tools. Rob had come in quietly and was sitting in the other chair.

'What—what are you doing here?' Laura managed. They hadn't seen much of Rob in the past week. He was out early and home late. At first, Laura had been concerned, and then angry. He had offered not one whit of explanation. Stacey, she thought, hating the idea.

'Shivering in fear,' he said placidly.

'You haven't shivered since you were five years old,' she told him as she went about picking up her tools. There was no assistant on duty; things had changed remarkably with the introduction of electric power in the office. But don't let that get you off the track, Laura warned herself.

'Actually, it was on my seventh birthday,' he corrected.

'What was on your—what are you talking about?'

'Shivering in fear,' he chuckled. 'You gave that young lady a very forceful dressing down. My tooth hurts, so I came to the dentist.'

'Oh?'

'That was about as noncommittal as one word can get, Laura. I beg your pardon—Dr Lackland. Are you related to that English King John Lackland who was so mean?'

'His name was Plantagenet, and I'm a direct descendant,' she snapped. 'In my family, he's called *Good* King John. That Robin Hood fellow wasn't all that nice, but it's only the winners who write the history books. Open your mouth. Which tooth is it?'

Rob made gargling noises, trying to talk with his mouth open while his finger pointed. Laura snapped on her examination light, picked up her mirror and pick, and had a look. From one side to the other, top and bottom, he had the most perfect teeth she had ever seen. Of course he would have, she thought. That's what money does for children!

'Are you sure it's that one?' She tapped the offender with her pick.

'Yes, the very one. Very painful, Doctor.' She looked again, carefully. There was not a thing wrong with the tooth. Perhaps if she had an X-ray machine she might— but that was idle dreaming. When one doesn't even have electricity it's useless to have an X-ray unit. On the other hand, Mr Robert Carlton was becoming noted in the Lackland family for his teasing. A test of her skills?

'Ah yes, Mr Carlton,' she mused as she searched around the tray for her most impressive drill, her largest hypodermic needle. 'A terrible problem. I can pull it if you wish; or I can drill and see if we can save it? It shouldn't take more than an hour or so!'

'Is it really that bad, Doctor?' Robert Carlton, tycoon, had suddenly become just another patient, with all a patient's fears. It was almost impossible for Laura to hide the smile that twitched at the corner of her mouth.

'No, it isn't. There's not a darn thing wrong with your teeth. Not a thing. So suppose you just tell me what the devil you're up to?'

Rob sat up, keeping a suspicious eye on that hypodermic needle. Laura set the tools back on the tray. 'Time is what I'm up to,' he said warily. 'There's only another two weeks until the stockholders meet at Carltonworld headquarters. Things are piling up and there's lots of work needing my hand. And I need your decision. Made up your mind yet?'

'I'm sorry, I haven't,' she apologised. 'I've been very busy. Emerald and I have talked the situation over half a dozen times, but—— You'll just have to bear with me, Robert.'

Yes, you liar, her conscience screamed at her. You and Emerald have talked it over—and agreed within the first ten minutes on what to do about the whole affair. So why am I so unwilling to tell him? Because, if I do, he'll pack up and leave, and that will be the end of everything! But there hasn't been an *everything* to be the end of, her conscience continued. He treats you like a sister. To be honest, he treats you and Emerald as if you were the same age and had the same worth in his eyes! And that really makes you mad, doesn't it, Dr Lackland?

'Shut up!' she muttered.

'What?'

'I said—I forget what I said,' she stammered.

'You look worried, Laura. Why not come out by the pool with me and tell me about it?'

'I can't, Robert, I really can't. I don't have a worry— I have a concern.' She scrubbed her hands, dried them, and walked over to the desk in the corner.

'Maybe you could explain that to me—the difference between a concern and a worry.'

'No, I can't,' she said crossly. 'Oh—I'm sorry. I shouldn't bark at you. The situation is, they've found my replacement. They've found a nice young man from Baltimore who's coming down to take my place. There's lots to be done, and—you know, I really hate to leave. We've enjoyed Saba—the people, the land—and everything. Are partings always so difficult?'

'I suppose they are,' he comforted. 'Where will this young man work?'

'Dr Liverman, Stephen Liverman,' she added. 'I decided to lease him this place. I don't want to sell it—we all love it too much for that. But this programme of fill-ins from Stateside has only three more years to run. There's a Sabian in training now in San Francisco. He's committed himself to come back home and work throughout the Antilles. He graduates in two years, and wants an additional year with some established dentist. So now I have to get all the records in shape, all the patients' charts up to date, all the leasehold material sorted out——' She turned around and offered him a real smile, dimples and all. 'You know, Robert, I'm the worst record-keeper who ever graduated from school. I don't know beans about systems, I'm not very orderly. On top of that, I can't keep house and I don't know how to cook.'

She leaned back in her swivel chair and fluffed her hair back up off her neck. 'You know, a long time ago there was a man named Charlie Flinders. Charlie asked me to marry him, and I turned him down. I don't think he'll ever know what a lucky escape he had!'

'When was that, Laura?' She was daydreaming. Dear little Charlie. It had been years since she even thought of his name.

'Laura?'

'What?' The tone of Rob's voice snapped her back to reality.

'When was all this that Charlie whosits asked you to marry him?' His fingers were drumming on the top of the desk. If I didn't know better I'd say he was angry, thought Laura.

'Charlie? Charlie Flinders? It was ages ago. It just didn't sound right—Laura Flinders. Does that sound for real to you?'

'Good God, is that why you turned him down? Because the name didn't sound right?'

'Well, for goodness' sake, Robert, we were both only ten years old at the time!' All the air and anger rushed out of him like a balloon that has just been pricked by a needle. He was smiling when he collapsed into a chair.

'You really give me a hard time, Laura Lackland,' he mused. 'Some day I'm going to do something about that.'

'Oh? Is that a promise or a threat? Should I hold my breath until you decide?'

'Look at me, woman!' he ordered.

'I *can't* do that. I have to take all these notes off these scraps of paper and put them in the proper forms.'

'Look at me, lady!' It was impossible to avoid it. He turned her chair around in his direction and lifted her chin up with his index finger. 'Watch my lips. You are a smart, good-looking lady, with a lot of courage and a great deal more stubbornness. Now, I can hire someone to keep house for me, and I'm a pretty good cook myself.'

'I—so what are you saying, Robert?'

'I'm saying I want you to marry me, Laura.'

'If this is where I say, "My goodness, you've surprised me," then I'm saying it,' she whispered. 'I—I had no idea. I'm—you've totally overwhelmed me. I—don't know what to say, I honestly don't.'

Rob pulled her up to her feet and held her hands. 'You never even noticed? What a blow *that* is to the male ego!' The famous Carlton smile lit up his face. Laura's heart hammered; her brains ran around in little circles.

'I don't mean to put you down, Robert. I—I think a very great deal of you, you must know that. But it—I have so much to do—I have to talk with others, too—I—what about Stacey?'

'Stacey has never been any part of my plans. Forget her. Do you want a rain-check, Laura? A chance to think it over?'

'You're not angry with me?'

'Providing this doesn't take as long as your business decisions, no, I'm not angry. Did I tell you I love you?'

'I—don't remember. Everything is so confusing. Do you?'

'I do,' he assured her.

'I think—I've never been in love before, Robert. I feel—excited.' And remember how easy it is for him to cast off one woman for another, Laura told herself cautiously.

'Maybe it's because you haven't had lunch,' he chuckled. 'Come on. I wouldn't want you to confuse love with indigestion.'

'But I—still have all this paperwork, Robert. I *have* to get it done.'

'Of course you do,' he agreed. He picked up a sample from each of the two stacks she had on the desk. 'That's all it takes? Move these numbers and these notes to the charts in this other pile—that doesn't sound too difficult. When's the last time you posted the charts?'

'I don't know,' she sighed. 'Six months, maybe?'

'There's a society for people like you.' Rob shook his head ruefully.

'What's it called?'

'The Procrastinators Society of America. And they have vacancies. Put all that stack in that big envelope, and put this other stack in this one——' He pushed her along until every bit of paper had disappeared from the desk. 'And now you stand up and say I'd love to lunch with you today, love.'

'I'd love lunch, love,' she murmured. 'But will it get the charts done?'

'It's like an incantation. It gets you a meal, and it also gets the papers done. Up, woman!'

'I—yes, sir.'

'Belle!' called Rob as he dragged Laura after him around the house. The older woman stuck her head out of the kitchen doorway. 'I'm taking Laura out to lunch. Be back some time.'

'Can I come? Can I?' Emerald squeezed by Belle and tore out after them. 'Please Rob—Mr Carlton!'

'Not this time,' he said, and winked at her. 'This is it, Emerald.'

'You mean you're going to ask her?'

'Shush! The walls have ears.'

'You're a terrible actor, Rob. And I can't go?'

'Of course not. This isn't a spectator sport. Scoot! Go do homework, or pester Belle——'

'Or clean up your room,' Laura intervened. 'That ought to take the rest of the weekend.'

'Spoilsport,' her daughter mourned. 'You'll get yours one of these days!'

'I hope so,' quipped Laura, then blushed. 'We'd better be going, Mr Carlton. Wherever we're going.'

Their destination was the Windwardside Guest House, a lovely rambling old inn, red-roofed like everything else on the island, standing just a few yards away from the cliffs that dropped straight down to the sea. From the windows of each of its four rooms there was a most magnificent view both south and eastward, across the silent sea. Outside, crowded into a corner of the garden, was something new—the white-painted round dish of a satellite antenna.

'You mean that Carltonworld has leased the whole place?' gasped Laura. 'And put in its own communication system? Why, that's like—I don't know what that's like, do I?' For the first time she had run up against Rob Carlton on his own turf. He seemed a different man, and she was not sure that she liked the change. There was a mournful sound in her voice. He recognised it, classified it, and took action.

'And this is my principal travelling secretary, Paul Mason. My senior secretary is Mrs Mary Saitemore. She can't travel, but she *can* hold the business together in New York. Paul, Dr Lackland has an administrative problem. Would you take care of it for her?'

Paul Mason was a middle-aged man with an interesting face. Not handsome by any means, but each little wrinkle and crevice in that face bespoke travel and knowledge and adventure. His eyes sparkled as if life were still an adventure, and he introduced Laura to two young ladies. They listened to her stammered statement, nodded, and applied efficiency and order to Laura's absent-minded system of operation.

Paul Mason looked at his watch and took Laura's arm. 'You can safely leave the problem to them. Mr Carlton expects you to join him for lunch in two and a half minutes.'

'Does he now?' Listen to that, Laura Lackland. Lunch in two and a half minutes. Snap to! Is that the way a tycoon's wife must live? To the minute. Up on the wall over the secretaries' desk she had noted in passing a typed agenda of Robert's day. Time, place, particulars, so the Corporation would always know where its head is, was, or would be. Dazzled by it all, and the muted hum of business machines, she followed docilely as Paul Mason led her out into the garden. Where a table has been prepared before him? Is that heresy or plain truth? she asked herself. He is truly king here!

Rob got up from the table, still holding a handful of papers, and kissed her cheek. 'No trouble, Paul?'

'No, of course not. The papers will be ready by four o'clock.' They both consulted their watches. One of the rites of the Church of Business? Laura sank down into her chair, suddenly realising how tired she was, how poorly fitted she was to be sharing a portion of Robert's life.

'This bit about the factory in Illinois,' he said, passing a paper to his secretary. 'Offer them twenty-two million. Up it another million for a fast transfer. This other one, the production from the Thailand plant, is not satisfactory. Ask for an explanation.' Ask for an explanation? Bring the guilty rascal in, Laura thought, and give him a fair trial before we hang him! 'And now, Laura, there's time for lunch.'

'How nice.' She couldn't help the meanness of her voice, the coolness of her look. I wasn't on the schedule, she told herself, so how can he have time for me? Well, of course, everybody has to eat. I don't suppose they catalogue with whom he eats!

He waved a hand, and a waiter brought the lunch. No waiting for an order, no choices for the guest. Her plate contained green salad, vegetables, thin slices of ham in pineapple sauce, and she had a teacup of coffee. All so elegant. Laura hated pineapple sauce.

'Lovely place up here.' Rob introduced the weather as a safe subject, she noted. 'Very windy, though. Wind blows all the time.'

'That's why they call it Windwardside,' she said quietly, as she tried to rescue pieces of the lovely ham from among the carnage of the sauce.

'You don't care for the meal?'

'Oh—no. It's lovely.' Lying about meals is not necessarily a major sin, Laura, but watch out! Am I using the wrong fork? They don't teach etiquette to dental students!

'You're very quiet. What's the matter?' Rob reached across the little table and touched her hand. It was the same flesh, the same man who had touched her before—but the result was not the same. He only seemed to be—half present. Some large part of him was listening to the little buzzers that made noises behind him. Occasionally he would stop to read something from the computer that stood to his right.

'I—don't know,' she stammered. 'You seem to have everything here. It must be awfully expensive.'

'At our level of business, a penny saved isn't always a good idea,' he chuckled. 'The name of the game is keep ahead of the opposition, and that requires instant information. All this stuff will pay for itself within two weeks or so.'

'It must have taken you a long time to learn all this—to become an executive?'

'Not too long, Laura. Big business is like sports—the fundamentals can be learned quickly. The *real* trouble is that a large industry tends to promote people from within who are amenable to the boss's ideas, so as a result we gradually accumulate near the top a bunch of industrious people who haven't any imagination. We promote them beyond their capabilities, keep them because they're on *our* side, and eventually, without new blood, the whole thing runs down. Some of the biggest corporations in the world today are running on momentum, not skill. And that's my lecture for the day.'

'But I——' Laura wanted to argue, but was afraid. Argument would expose her abysmal ignorance, as well as her parochial biases. But there was *one* thing she had to know.

'I suppose there are times when you have to make hard decisions? When you have to choose, say, between the old, familiar things you love, and the new track of things?'

'All the time, Laura. It's just like teeth—some of them have to go.'

'And you would have to be ruthless about that?'

'Like pruning a tree,' he agreed.

'Which means there isn't a great deal you wouldn't do to make Carltonworld go?'

'Not a great deal,' he agreed casually. 'Would you like to take another tour of the island with me?'

'Oh, you can't do that, Robert! Your schedule——'

'Ah, you saw that,' he laughed. 'Just remember, that's for the workers, Laura. The man on top can deviate any time he wants to.'

'Yes, I see that,' she replied. 'But you have things to do, and *I* have a family to gather up, and there's going to be a storm.'

'Is there really? I don't have much time for weather.'

'Around here, it's something you always keep in mind,' she said. 'Like the Ten Commandments. Is there some way I could get home?'

'Of course. Paul will find someone to run you back to Hell's Gate. Where the devil did they get those names?'

'All invented by seamen of the past,' she told him. 'Some were saints, some were sinners, and most of them were pirates. Paul will find me a driver?'

'Yes, love.' He rose when she did, and offered her a kiss that missed her lips and found her nose. Totally unsatisfactory, Laura told herself fiercely. When a girl has to manoeuvre to be sure her face is in the right position for kissing, something's wrong with the world! I'd better find Paul and see if he can get me home. 'I'll be over for dinner,' Rob called after her as she deserted him.

She found Paul, and he, amiable man that he was, made everything the boss had promised come true. Well, some of the things.

Stacey Mantoff was pacing back and forth at the door of the guest house as Laura came out. Her bags were scattered around her.

'Don't think you've won anything!' the blonde spat. 'The game isn't over yet—you'll find out the hard way. He'll find a way to dump you, you little fool, and when he does I'll be there to warm his bed!'

When the jeep came for her, Laura climbed in, dazed by the emotional attack, and not a little worried.


'How come you go to lunch with that nice man, and you come home hungry?' Belle bustled around the kitchen. Laura's taste for ham had been titillated, but far from satisfied. The two huge ham sandwiches Belle set in front of her seemed more the thing.

'Pineapple sauce,' Laura sighed.

'Ah. He gotta learn.'

'I know. Where's Emerald?'

'She out by the pool with the Van Hooten boys.'

'I think I'll take these sandwiches along, and read my latest thriller.'

'You don't gotta do all that paperwork, like you said?'

'Belle, Mr Carlton is taking care of it. Did you know he has leased the whole——'

'I know all about it, Missy. You weren't so locked up in your work to hear the gossip, you'd know too.'

'I suppose so. What are you going to do this afternoon?'

'I gonna put my feet up and nap,' Belle responded. 'You needs me, you just call.'

Laura picked up her tray and went outside. The Van Hooten boys, four of them, were stair-step children, the youngest eight, the oldest sixteen. Emerald fitted right in the middle. *And that's another thing I've got to do,* Laura told herself as she pulled a chair back away from the splashing war going on in the pool. *I've got to convince Emerald that she's a girl.* She watched the five of them at play. It was a comfort. *That little girl, running and jumping and laughing, that's my daughter,* she thought. *The doctors said she would never walk, that long time ago, and look at her now!*

For just a moment, Laura allowed herself the luxury of pride. That was something that Laura Lackland had done—taken the baby who might never walk and fulfilled the promise she had made to her sister Anne, to see that Emerald became a normal, well-loved child. There was a satisfaction to that. There was a satisfaction, too, as she bit into the ham sandwiches. So, even though the book was terrible, on balance the day had not been too bad.

She held the book up before her as a cover—to avoid being invited into the pool play. Behind the disguise she reviewed things. Robert Carlton, a prize of a man, who wanted to marry her. A man chased by hundreds of women, none of whom had managed to pull off the *coup*. He's a safe, warm, lovable man, who throws women away when he's tired of them. *What am I doing, loving a man like that?*

'Mama? Mama!' Laura snapped to. The boys had gone, and Emerald was shaking her shoulder, not too gently.

'What is it, dear? I must have dropped off. Why wake me up?'

'Because the storm is coming! Belle says fold up the light chairs and bring them in the house, and hurry up about it or she'll be out here with her broom and we'll both be in trouble.' The child stopped to take a breath.

'And that's why I woke you up. You're sitting on the only chair that's left.'

'Now, haven't *you* been energetic!' Fully aware now, Laura got up and exchanged hugs with her daughter. The pair of them together carried the chair into the kitchen and then through to the storage cupboard. Laura went on to the front door, which faced eastward, and looked out. Massive black clouds towered skyward. The gentle wind had gone, replaced by a tiger-tail of a breeze that whipped this way and that, rattling the old trees, stripping bushes of their leaves, shaking at the windows. 'Not good,' she muttered as she shut the door carefully and went back to the kitchen.

'If it wasn't so late in the season, I'd swear it was a hurricane, Belle,' she said worriedly. 'We'd better check all the doors and windows.'

'I done that already in the house, Missy. Got my radio out. The man says tropical depression—sounds bad.' The older woman flipped on the light switch. It was only four o'clock, but the storm was creating an early night. The electric lamp glowed assuringly.

'I'll go check your office,' Emerald promised, and was off before either of them could stop her. The back screen door was snatched out of the child's hands, and banged viciously against the doorframe several times before Laura could rescue it.

'Got to get the hurricane supplies,' muttered Belle. They were stored in a special place in the hall cupboard. A few cans of food, a large water-bottle to be filled immediately with fresh water, spare flashlights, an extra kerosene lamp, matches. All the things that a person living under the Equator kept readily to hand—for just the sort of storm they faced.

Laura waited at the kitchen door until Emerald returned from the other building. 'It's starting to rain,' the little girl reported. 'Big drops, Mama.'

'Don't worry,' her mother assured her. 'This house was built to withstand hurricane winds. We'll be all right.'

'But how about Mr Carlton? He'll miss his supper.'

'Don't worry, child. Mr Carlton is a grown man, he can take care of himself.'

'Did he ask you, Mama?'

'Ask me—oh, that. Yes, dear. What do *you* think?' asked Laura.

'I know it's not my business, Mama, but I like him. He's a nice man. He doesn't treat me like a—like a cripple.'

'Hey, now!' Laura pulled the child over between her knees and hugged her. 'Of course it's your business, and Belle's, too. If I marry him, you know that means he'll be your father.'

'I'll be darned,' Emerald said blissfully. 'I always wanted a father, Mama. But we've been happy, me and you and Belle——'

'You and I and Belle,' Laura corrected automatically. 'Yes, we've been happy, haven't we? But you'd like to have a father? This particular man? We don't know him all that well, you know. Suppose I married him and we found out he didn't like peanut butter and jelly?'

'Oh, wow! Nobody's that stiff, Mama. Belle, did you know that Mama and Mr Carlton——'

'I knows all about everything, child. Would you believe, he knows Missy don't have no family—'cepting me. He come and asked *me* first!'

'Oh no, Belle, he didn't!'

'Yeah, he sure did, Missy. He surely did,' Belle assured her.

'And what did you tell him?'

'I told him nothin' but the truth. I told him you was a stubborn, opinionated woman, who never had no chance to be young and happy.'

'Belle, you didn't!'

'Yes, I did, Missy. And you, Miss Emerald, you stop laughing at your ma. Stop this minute, or I gonna whack you little round bottom for you! Did you wash you hands? Can't sit at *my* table with dirty hands! Git!'

Emerald disappeared down the hall, trailing a trainload of giggles behind her. 'Sassy little miss,' grumbled Belle. 'Jus' like you used to be. Did you wash *you* hands?'

Laura let it all pass. If I ever get to be ninety, she told herself, Belle will still be treating me like a child. And why not? Talk about *me* having no childhood, how about Belle? She was working as a maid for Grandpa Lackland when she was fourteen! Compared to her, I've lived high up, in the cream! 'I did, honestly,' she said.

The old black woman pulled out a chair and sat down, something she seldom did. Busy, to Belle, meant moving around, doing. 'I get tired, Missy. Tireder than I ought. I—you was my child, little Laura. And Emerald's my child. And I jus' hope I gonna last long enough to see *your* child. Missy, he a good man, but all men is hard to live with, you know. He got his own ways, he got his own thing to do. Lovin' is what men do when they come home after the day. But lovin' is what women do all day and all night—you remember that, now. I ain't gonna say another word. You wanna marry that man, I gonna be right there at the church. You hear?'

'I—guess that makes it unanimous, Belle,' smiled Laura. 'And you needn't worry, you'll be around a long time yet. But I mean to tell him, he has to marry us all.'

'Oh, I don't think he want to have an old woman like me around his fancy house in the big city,' Belle said sombrely. 'I got some things you grandpa left me, and

I got some money saved, maybe I go back to the island and see what happen to all those friends I had.'

Laura moved around the table and put her arms around Belle. 'I mean it,' she said fiercely. 'If you aren't going to him, then neither am I. I am your daughter; you are my mother. You think I want my mother running around the beaches of Haiti, making eyes at all those men, and getting in trouble?'

'Go on with you, girl!' Belle choked on her words as if something were obstructing her throat. Her eyes glistened. 'All right, Missy. I do it if you do it!'

'That's better, love. We'd better eat early, just in case, shall we? Emerald! That girl has more excuses for *not* washing, and takes more time *doing* it, than any girl I've ever known. Sit still, Belle, I'll serve your plate.'

'I know one or two jus' like that,' the old woman said as she reached for her spoon.

'What have I done now?' Emerald complained as she came back into the kitchen.

'Nothing—yet!' her mother told her. 'Belle has just been reminding me what a difficult child *I* was to raise. Sit down and eat your soup.'

'Did she ever whack you, Mama?'

'No, but she threatened. She used to keep an old ping-pong paddle in the kitchen, and every time I misbehaved she threatened terrible things.'

'But she never whacked you?'

'No.' Laura laughed in reminiscence. 'I think she really would have, but it takes two, you know. There's always the whacker and the whackee. She never could catch me. How's that soup?'

'That good soup, Missy,' Belle approved. 'See, you *can* cook if you put you mind to it.'

'Yes, surely,' chuckled Laura. 'Me and Mr Campbell can do wonders with a soup can.'

'Mr Campbell and I.' Her daughter grinned at her, happy to catch her in the middle of an error. Laura raised her index finger and made an imaginary mark in the air.

'One for you, baby.' The wind took that moment to raise a ruckus. The whole house shook. The wooden shutters over the windows strained and creaked. There was a clatter out at the back.

'The garbage can,' Emerald conceded. 'I forgot it.'

The electric light on the table began to flicker. The wind took another massive bash at the house, then fell silent. In the eerie moment before it began again, the light flickered, flashed, and went out.

'I'll get the lamp lit,' said Emerald. She got up from the table, then froze, as did the other two. Something out at the back was creaking and straining more heavily than the house. Something out there was swaying in the wild wind. Something out there had come loose, and——

The crash was loud enough to shatter their calm. Emerald ran for her mother, sheltering in her arms. Something out there had just fallen on the back of the house.

'That was glass breaking,' said Belle. 'Your studio. The roof done bust, or somethin'. I'll get the lamp.'

In a matter of seconds the soft yellow light of the kerosene lamp relieved the dismal gloom. 'Let's go look in your studio,' a revived Emerald proposed.

'Nonsense!' Laura said sharply. 'Leave everything here. Let's all go to the bathroom—quick!'

'But I don't need to go,' Emerald complained.

'You need to,' Laura explained. 'This storm is worse than I thought. The safest place to be in a hurricane is in the bathroom. All the fixtures are firmly fastened to something deep in the ground—pipes and things like that.

If the whole house were to blow away, the bathroom would still be left, so that's where we're going. And you can hide under the sink. Right now!'

# CHAPTER NINE

THE STORM broke just after midnight, and the moon harried its last tattered wisps westward towards Costa Rica and the mainland. Emerald was fast asleep on the floor of the bathroom, her hands still holding on to the pipes of the washbowl.

'I'll put the little lady to bed, Belle. You should go, too.' Laura's shoulders ached from the long hours huddling in the corner, but she tried to put a good face on things. Belle had lost her smile, and with the loss she had aged tremendously. She puffed to her feet, and took a couple of experimental steps.

'You go ahead, Missy. I gonna check around the house first.'

'Keep out of the studio,' Laura whispered fiercely. 'I'll look there in the morning!'

'Awright, Missy. Here, let me help pick her up. She a big heavy girl, that one. Pretty soon she gonna grow bigger than both of us.'

'And smarter,' Laura returned softly. How could she *not* be smarter? she thought. Look what Belle and I have done with *our* lives.

'Where that Mr Carlton?' grumbled Belle as she helped balance Emerald in Laura's arms, with the child's head resting on her mother's shoulder. 'One thing about men, they always around when you don't want them, but when you *need* one—ha!'

'It's not that bad,' Laura soothed as they went down the hall. 'He had a great deal of work to do—and I suppose the wind was worse up at the guest house than it was down here. Otherwise I'm sure he would come.'

'You sure got a lot of believin', Missy. They up there at Windwardside, all cosy and snug, him and that Miss Mantoff. What kind of name is that for a woman? She got claws, that one. You don't wanna wrestle her, b'lieve me.'

'She's gone, Belle, for heaven's sakes. Go to bed!'

Laura could hear Belle clattering around the house as Emerald stirred slightly. 'Mama?'

'Yes, Mama's right here, love. And here you are in your own bed. Close those eyes again, everything's all right.' The little girl smiled up at her, closed her eyes, and rolled over on her stomach. Laura stayed with her for a few moments, smoothing the top sheet and the blanket innumerable times. In the background she could hear Belle still mumbling to herself, until the old woman went into her own room and closed the door behind her.

Laura followed suit, only when she sat down on the edge of her bed to unfasten her shoes she was stuck with a dream. Stacey Mantoff. She might have left, but was it over or will she still be trying it on with my Robert? she wondered. But *I'm* the one he asked to marry him. He's known Stacey for years and years, but he asked *me* to marry him. She pulled her knees up, wrapped her arms around them, and rocked back and forth for a few gleeful minutes, then fell back on the bed and was instantly asleep.

Emerald woke her up. The child was sitting cross-legged at the bottom of Laura's bed, singing under her breath. 'Did I wake you up, Mama?' she asked.

Laura shook her head as she sat up. 'Oh, no, I'm never bothered by people singing at the foot of my bed. Were you *trying* to wake me up?'

'Me? Belle said that would be a cruel thing, after all the work you did last night. No, I wouldn't do a thing like that. I wanted to ask you——'

'If I don't get to the bathroom, love, at least one of us is going to be embarrassed! Go on down to the kitchen. I'll get dressed and come myself. Is Belle——'

'Oh, she's been up for hours. Breakfast is ready. It's almost nine o'clock. I've never seen you sleeping so late.'

Laura slid out from under the blanket, stretched, and whirled her daughter up for a hug. 'This may be the last time,' she chuckled. 'I do believe you've put on ten pounds this last week. One more, and I won't be able to hold you! And I slept late because I was up late last night with pleasant company. All females—Belle and you and I and the storm.'

'I thought storms were men!'

'Not in the Indian tradition,' Laura laughed. 'Thunder is a man. He stomps and roars and snarls. Storm is a woman. She moves the world and shapes it. Hey, those Indians were right! Off you go, baby.'

Emerald jumped down, performed a pirouette, and ran down the hall. Laura watched with thankful eyes. Run, jump, laugh, she thought. And, in a couple of years, a visit to a plastic surgeon and those scars will be gone. Emerald Lackland, star of stage and screen, weds multi-millionaire. That dark blob in the picture is her mother, hanging anxiously on to the edge of the crowd! God, what a thought!

She brushed her teeth vigorously, as a sort of penance, then threw on an old pair of slacks and an old green blouse. It had once been white, but had not survived being washed in the same load as one of Emerald's little supposedly colour-fast dresses. Laura smiled at the memory, and the sight staring back at her from the bathroom mirror. Her hair just *refused* to take any part in the organisational effort going forward, so she abandoned the effort with hair and face, and walked happily to the kitchen. If she paused just the slightest in front of the door to Robert's room, it was probably because her shoe was coming untied. Or so she told herself.

''Bout time you was up.' Belle was at the stove, as usual, making scrambled eggs. 'They was two, three patients. I sent them all away—told them the doctor had to clean up the storm damage. Nobody complained. How could they, gettin' free service from a *bona fide* dentist?'

'What kind of dentist?' asked Emerald, her mouth half stuffed with dry cereal.

'A *real* one,' Belle answered. 'Come on now, Missy— eat! You the most finicky eater I ever saw! We gotta get ten, maybe fifteen pounds on you do you mean to keep you man.'

'Belle, please!' protested Laura. 'You embarrass me. I don't *have* a man.'

'So you eat anyway, and maybe you get one,' the housekeeper insisted. 'This here family *need* a man.' She set an overloaded plate in front of Laura, who groaned at the size of it, then did her best. They all meant well for her, she knew, as she did for them.

Half-way through the eggs, they heard the rattle-bang of Rob's jeep coming down the drive. Laura's heart skipped a beat, but she sat still. Emerald lacked the control. The minute she heard the noise she was up and running for the front door.

'Rob!' they heard her shout. 'You should have seen! Something fell over on top of the house, and the wind blew like crazy, and I went to sleep on the bathroom floor because that's where you ought to hide in a hurricane and——' The joy seemed to fade suddenly. 'Why did you bring her?'

'Had to, little bit,' he chuckled. They were coming back into the house, down the corridor. At the kitchen door he stopped. 'Morning, all,' he greeted them. 'We had a great deal of trouble at the guest house last night, and the kitchen's out of order. On top of that, the storm cancelled air flights, and Stacey was stuck for another day. I hope you don't mind that I brought her along to see if we could both chisel some breakfast?'

Belle gave him a glare of sullen disapproval. Emerald, feeling the nuance of the situation, suddenly discovered she had to go to the bathroom. Which left Laura out on a limb. Fuming inside, smiling outside, she stood up to greet them.

'Of course we don't mind. Everyone has to help everyone else in a shipwreck. Please sit down. Belle will make some more scrambled eggs—I think—won't you, Belle?' It was the special little pleading that did it. Belle nodded and turned her back on them all. Emerald came to the door, was surprised to see that peace had broken out, and walked around to her chair and her unfinished breakfast.

'What a quaint little place,' said Stacey, looking around the crowded kitchen. 'You don't have a dining-room—er—Doctor?'

Laura swallowed hard. Her normally volatile temper had become super-heated these last few weeks. She wanted to shout at this woman, and beat her madly about the head and shoulders. No woman has the right to be all dressed up, with her face done and her hair combed, not at—good lord, almost ten in the morning! she thought. And I got that *Doctor* business, chum. It was *last* week I was Dr Lackland. *This* week I'm a woman, fixing to fight, as Grandpa Lackland always said!

'We got scrambled eggs,' Belle announced belligerently. 'What kind you want?'

'Scrambled.' Rob grinned. He could sense the female war being waged all around him, but was not quite sure of its depth. 'With sausages?'

'I jus' happen to have three or four sausage left over,' said Belle, still in her war-is-declared attitude. 'What kind eggs you want, Miss Mantoff?'

'Oh, heavens, I don't eat eggs for breakfast!' Stacey shuddered. 'That leads to unsightly bulges in unfortunate places. And then there's the cholesterol, you know.' Her dainty little hands traced a demonstration tour along her own svelte little curves. 'A piece of toast, some coffee, a little fruit?'

'That's what we got,' Belle said firmly. 'A little fruit. That Mr Carlton, he ate all the fruit in the house night before last. Left us only one grape.'

'Belle!' Laura admonished. The old lady shrugged her shoulders and went back to work. Emerald had been watching her contest, her head swinging from side to side like a spectator at a tennis match.

'And what are you grinning at, young lady?' demanded Laura.

'Me?' the child asked innocently. 'Mama, I have to go to school, and I'll be late, and you'll have to write me a note.'

'I'm declaring a holiday,' Laura announced. 'In celebration of—well, everything nice that's happened lately. But it's only a holiday from school. You still have to do your swimming exercises.'

'I brought back your charts and notes,' Rob commented. 'Everything finished, all ship-shape. Say, did we have a stormy time last night! Is there any little thing around here that needs fixing?'

'Oh, for goodness' sake, Rob! You and I were going into town today. You *know* I have to go shopping.' Stacey gave everyone a bored look, and nibbled disdainfully at the toast Belle had put before her. Rob examined his loaded plate with appreciation, then took a sample.

'I said I'd take you, so I will,' he said between bites. 'But first I want to help fix any little thing that might have been damaged during the storm.'

'In that case, we got us a little thing that busted.' Belle was at her most aggressive. 'You know that big tower thing with the electrical?'

'The windmill?' asked Rob. 'Get turned around, did it?'

'Got blowed down,' Belle said in her favourite 'Voice of Doom' imitation.

'And it knocked a hole right through Mama's studio, Rob, and broke all the roof, and we don't dare go in there yet until Mama says we can, because there's glass around and everything.'

'I don't believe it!' said Robert. He pushed back his chair and walked out back, to the edge of the swimming pool. Within minutes he was back. 'I believe it,' he mourned. 'Almost as if it was aimed for the house. Missed the swimming pool by a hair. I'll have to—— Van Hooten, the very man! Where does he live, Emerald?'

'Up the hill, just across the road. The house with the green door and a lot of boys outside.'

'Can't miss it. I'll just amble up there now.'

'Finish you breakfas', man!' ordered Belle.

'But, Rob, my shopping!' Stacey wailed.

'Belle, put my plate back on the stove, Stacey, find something to amuse yourself with, and I'll be back before you can say *Stanislaus Zwielskinski*.'

'Who?' Emerald shouted.

'No orders for me?' shouted Laura.

'For you—you just sit and wait, lady. And pine for me.'

'Go on with you!' chided Belle. All the women watched while he swaggered out of the door. Renaissance

Man, Laura thought. He can do anything. But it was *his* tower that fell down! Has my hero feet of clay?

'And just what is there to do in this—place?' Stacey asked in that sweet, honeyed voice of hers.

'Well, we have the swimming pool,' Laura told her. 'There aren't many on the island. You could paddle around—I'll loan you a suit.'

Stacey glared at Laura's five foot six, comparing it to her own compact five foot nothing. 'No, thank you. I didn't come to make a public spectacle of myself.'

'So then you could sit by the pool and read,' Laura replied. I don't have time for you today, Miss Bountiful.

'C'mon, Emerald,' Belle commanded. 'We get you in you swimsuit, and you can show Miss Mantoff what a clever girl you are.' The pair of them went off to do just that.

'I don't think I'd care to look,' Stacey told Laura. 'All those horrible scars! I would think you'd do your best to hide them.'

'Pick on me all you want,' Laura gritted through clenched teeth, 'but don't say a bad word about my daughter, or I'll have *several* to say to you!' She pushed back her chair and stood up. Stacey flinched, as if expecting more than a verbal assault. When nothing happened, she regained her courage.

'You know he's still mine,' she hissed. 'He has been, he is, and he will be. We had a wild time at the guest house last night!'

'I'm astonished by your imagination,' snapped Laura. 'All those lies must keep you happy, or you wouldn't keep repeating them. Smarten up, Staccy. I don't doubt you've been in his bed in the past, but it's *me* he wants in marriage. If he'd wanted you, he had ten years or more to propose, didn't he? Doesn't that tell you something? Nobody *buys* milk when the dairy is giving it away! You give the rest of womankind a bad name. Try the pool—but don't fall in, I just had it cleaned and sterilised!' With that, Dr Lackland marched smartly out of the kitchen, headed for her studio.

It wasn't as bad as she had expected; it was much worse. The tower had collapsed in such a fashion that the head, including the blades, the rotor and the generator, had slammed through the studio roof, spreading havoc as it went. More than half the paintings in hand were scratched or torn. Two were totally destroyed. Glass shards filled the floor. Laura walked over to the easel, stepping with care. Her last work, unfinished, was safe. She pulled the covering cloth over it and looked around again. 'Oh my!' was all she could think to say.

She heard Belle and Emerald go out of the back door, but it was one of those unconscious things that you do— you know deep down what is happening, but it doesn't float to the surface. *Laura's* surface mind was stunned! She couldn't decide whether to go for a broom, or sit down on the floor and cry. Luckily, the telephone rang before she committed herself. That's God calling, she told herself. He wants me to stop being so nasty to Stacey, and this is his object-lesson! Go answer the telephone, dummy. You're the only one in the house.

She took another quick look around the studio, then ran down the hall. Strangely enough, Robert's room was immaculate, everything in its place. Oh, me—disorganised! Laura thought. Look at that! When we're married, he'll make me sleep at attention! By now, the telephone sounded hoarse. She snatched up the instrument, and was completely surprised how clear the conversation sounded. The man could almost be in the next room, rather than in the middle of New York, a thousand miles away!

Rob came back in about an hour, whistling happily like one of the Seven Dwarfs. He could hear the noise as

Emerald splashed and Belle cheered—and presumably Stacey watched. But it was Laura he wanted. There was the sound of glass breaking from the direction of the studio. He went eagerly along the corridor, and there she was. Her back was to him as she swept the loose glass into piles. He walked over behind her and reached around to put his hands over her eyes.

'Guess who?'

'I'm in no mood for guessing games,' she snapped. Rob turned her around. Her face was white, glistening with perspiration. He had never seen her so pale, so much in the hands of controlled anger, and he tried to pass it off.

'We'll have a crew here tomorrow, and a new tower in the day after,' he said. She could almost taste the satisfaction in his voice. Rub your hands together, she commanded silently. He rubbed his hands together. 'But I don't know what I can do to repair these paintings. That's a lovely seascape, Laura and what's this?' He was at the easel, pulling the cloth cover back. 'Me?' He turned to smile at her, but got no response. 'Is that the way you see me, Laura?'

'Not any more,' she retorted, her face full of pain. 'I haven't finished it. I doubt if I will.'

'What is it, love?'

'Don't call me that!' she snarled. 'Don't you ever call me that again!'

'What have I done? At least give me a chance to defend myself!'

Laura took a deep breath, threw her broom in a corner, and walked over to face him. 'Stacey told me you two were lovers.'

'And you believe that?' He grabbed her shoulders and gave her a brief shake. She stood very still.

'Take your hands off me, please.' A cold command, with no feeling, neither love nor hate. For a second he refused. She made no struggle, and finally he moved his hands away, regretfully.

'You're condemning me for something Stacey claimed?'

'No!' she snapped at him. 'That isn't important. You're entitled to all the women you can catch—and I guess you've had your share, Robert.'

'Well, *what* then? I've a million things to do today.'

'I don't doubt you do, Robert. It wasn't only your windmill that collapsed last night, it was your whole deck of cards.'

'Explain!' he ordered.

'You proposed to me yesterday, Mr Carlton. You didn't need to, as it turns out, so you won't hold it against me if I respectfully decline your offer? I realise how much you've honoured me by asking, but——'

'Dear God, Laura, what the hell are you talking about?'

'I took a telephone call about twenty minutes ago, Mr Carlton. A Mr Marks, who claimed to be your brother-in-law. He asked me to give you a message.'

'Oh, brother!' sighed Robert. 'With relatives like him, who needs enemies? May I ask what the message was?'

'I made a note.' Laura took her little pad out of her pocket and flipped it open. 'He asked me if I were your secretary, and I told him I took orders from you, so I think he thought I worked for Carltonworld. The message goes something like this: You can give up your Saba plot. We've found an easier way to settle the problem of proxies. The will of Jacob Blake expressly left his entire estate to Emerald. He did so by using the phrase "Everything bequeathed to that child known as Emerald Blake Lackland, and who resided with my son and daughter-in-law." So whether or not Emerald was Jacob's granddaughter is not important. And Laura Lackland is appointed executor of the estate in the same sort of language. But there is some doubt that Miss Lackland is really the legal guardian, and our legal department is filing suit seeking to have her set aside. So please don't plan to marry the girl, or something else equally stupid. Your sister sends her love.'

She examined the pages of her notebook, as if looking for something else to tell him. Finally she snapped it closed, returned it to her pocket, and stood there, swaying back and forth, toe to heel, while her teeth nibbled on her lower lip. 'And that's the message, Mr Carlton.'

'Damn it, Laura, the man's an ass! Surely you don't believe I proposed marriage just to——'

'Just to get a favourable ruling in the stockholders' meeting?' she finished the sentence for him. 'You remember us having lunch at Windwardside? Do anything at all to save your company, that's what you said. High or low, sin or secret, you'd do it. Yes, Mr Carlton, I *do* believe you proposed marriage for that purpose. And you're lucky, aren't you? You don't have to follow up. You can take yourself and dear Miss Mantoff back to the big city where you'll be happy!'

Rob opened his mouth to say something, then thought better of it. Laura swallowed to clear a blocked throat, and continued, 'But don't think this ends our war, Mr Carlton. There's nothing more precious to me than my daughter Emerald. I'll fight you, using any underhanded trick I can find, because I *will not* let you have control of her!'

'So you believe all this nonsense,' he muttered. 'You *do* think I spent all last night in bed with Stacey? What a high opinion you have of me, Dr Lackland!'

'I call them as I see them, Mr Carlton. There are times I wish I could find my old Carlton doll to cuddle, and see faith and comfort in a man, but I've grown to be a cynical old maid. And I think that's all I have to say.

Now, I would like you and your mistress to pack up and get out of my house within the hour. Get off the island too, while you're at it. There's nothing on Saba for you.'

'You really mean it, don't you?' he muttered, still dazed by what he was hearing.

'I really mean it. Go now, please.'

'And never darken your door again?' he asked bitterly.

'And never darken my door. Go now, please.'

He stood there, feet spread apart, hands in pockets, shoulders slumping, with a grey look on his face. For one awful minute, Laura wanted to reach out to comfort him, but she managed to suppress the urge and the tears that threatened. Rob thought, pursing his lips in and out, and then he nodded.

'All right, Laura, if that's the way you want it. Goodbye, my love.' He turned on his heel and walked away. She heard the slamming of luggage lids as he packed, the deadly silence that followed his arrival at the poolside to collect his *real* lady love, and Emerald's scream. Later, the old jeep rattled and banged, but Laura didn't hear that. She was sitting on the floor, crying, her mind shattered into a million shards, like the glass from the window. I was happy in my little world, fast asleep, she thought. Why did *he* have to come into it and break down the walls? Now I'll never be able to seal them up again. *Goodbye, my love.* The pain was too much. Dr Laura Lackland rolled forward and beat her head against the cool cement floor, then fainted.

# CHAPTER TEN

THERE'S nothing about New York that I could like, Laura thought as she looked out of the window over a snow-bound city. The streets had been ploughed, but the big flakes had started to fall again. The pavements were massed with people fighting their way along. The streets of Manhattan were wall-to-wall cars, as if the island had become one massive car park, all stuck in place. February dullness hung over the city. The top floors of the World Trade Center were masked by the clouds.

Larry Hinton came into the room with a fistful of papers. Laura had always thought of lawyers in Mr Ladessy's image—old, warped, in frame but not in mind, shaggy. Larry Hinton, junior partner in Hymore, Hamson and Hinton, was sleek, polished and very sure of himself. And I ought to be honoured that one of the partners took time for me, instead of some inexperienced member of staff, she thought.

'All settled, Dr Lackland.' He showed her a mouthful of smile. All capped, she smiled to herself, with two laminated veneers. A good job. It made him more human, less like a superior being. She took the two sets of papers he handed her. 'I have little doubt that the Carltonworld suit will be thrown out of court. They have absolutely no case at all. Besides, they can hardly get on the court calendar in less than eighteen months. The subpoena they secured, requiring you to appear for a deposition, has been quashed. Now, to make you officially a stockholder, we have purchased in your name one share of Carltonworld. In addition, we have assessed your daughter's holdings, forty-three thousand, five hundred shares, and Judge Henderson has issued a writ confirming your right to vote with those shares. The secretary of the Carltonworld Corporation was notified by a personal service this morning. We will, of course, watch the course of the Carltonworld suit, and are prepared to take action in your name should anything transpire. And that, I believe, is that.' He leaned back in his chair and clasped his hands in front of him.

'I don't know how to thank you,' she murmured.

'No thanks necessary.' He waved a hand airily. 'You wouldn't know, but your Mr Ladessy gave me my first job. And, besides, when you see the size of our bill——' He stopped in the middle of the sentence, grinning.

'Then all I have to do is get to the RCA building,' Laura sighed.

'It's only across the street,' he chuckled, 'but you might need an hour to make it. Off you go. The meeting is due to start in—oh—forty-five minutes.' He rose and escorted her to the door. Outside his soundproof office, the air was filled with the clatter of typewriters, word processors, and other machinery. Laura walked between the rows of desks and boarded the express elevator. It dropped like a shot, leaving her stomach two floors behind her. Out on the pavement she stopped at the kerb for a moment, loving the soft feel of the huge flakes that filled her hair. She had been a Connecticut snow-child, but the year on tropical Saba had weakened her memories. Someone had shovelled a narrow walk across the street. She followed it, head down to watch her footing, between the lines of cars that glared at her. One of the drivers, resentful of her movement, leaned on his horn. Laura looked up and smiled at him, then continued on her way.

The offices of Carltonworld were on the thirty-eighth floor. When the elevator man tried to cram her into the machine marked 'Express' she fought her way back out, and waited for one that would stop at every floor. At least *those* can't go faster than ninety miles an hour, she told herself. But it was a long, tedious ride up thirty-eight stops. Thirty-eight steps to Karma? It's been five weeks since I've seen him. Will he be changed? Or perhaps by this time he'll have married Stacey Mantoff. Wouldn't they be a lovely pair? He doesn't deserve that. Or maybe he does!

The elevator doors opened on Carltonworld. Laura took a deep breath and stepped out. The floor carpets were ankle-deep beige. The reception desk was chrome and steel. The receptionist was steel, too—steel and pancake make-up. Laura had to display her single share certificate before the woman condescended to direct her. Straight ahead, through the hedge of potted ferns, turn left at the corridor, down four doors to the end.

*The end* was a large conference room, with a stage at one end, and a scattering of folding chairs, most of which were empty. Laura chose to stay at the back. Nervous bugs were eating at her stomach. All the rest of the people in the room looked exceedingly bored. And, within minutes, Robert would be there. She jumped at the voice over her shoulder. 'My goodness, the little country doctor, come all the way to New York!'

'All the way,' she agreed. Stacey Mantoff shrugged herself out of her mink coat and sat down in the next chair. Under the coat she was dressed in a form-fitting suit, made feminine because she was inside it. Laura hugged her own cotton coat closer. Under it she wore a plain old house dress. Perhaps I shouldn't have stayed in the old house outside Hempstead, she thought. For sure, I shouldn't have tried to clean the place up. I *should* have booked into the Algonquin, or the Hilton, or something like that, and bought myself a wardrobe full of warm clothes. Why? So I could demonstrate to Mr Carlton that I'm an even bigger fool than he thought?

'What brings you to the sacred halls?' Stacey was whispering. Laura said nothing, but displayed her stock-share.

'One?' The voice had turned shrill, loaded with derision.

'Yes, one,' Laura announced coolly, firmly. 'Just enough to give me a voice in the procedures. How many shares do *you* have?'

'Shares, my dear? How silly! I have a large voice in the procedures, you know. Robert's.'

'The day that *he* allows some woman to dictate will be a cool day in hell,' Laura returned. 'If I were you, I'd get the shares. They may not be so comfortable in bed, but they surely do a lot for a girl's confidence.'

The little round blonde's face turned ugly. Her fingers curled up like claws, threatening.

'And before anything else happens that you might not like,' Laura commented softly, 'please remember that I don't particularly like you, and that I hold a brown belt in karate.'

'You don't frighten me,' stuttered Stacey. 'I've got Robert. You can have all the karate belts you want!' She gathered up her coat and bag and stalked down to the very front row to find another seat.

Dragon-slaying, Laura chuckled to herself. One down, and the lord only knows how many more to go. Everyone in the room stopped talking. The five directors of the company had filed on to the stage. A moment later Robert came out and joined them at the table. The person in the centre, a heavy-set, elderly man, pounded a gavel twice. The woman to his right coughed and settled back in her chair. Laura was too engrossed to bother with the rest of them; she was studying Robert.

He slumped a little, in his separate chair at the corner of the long table. There were long deep worry-furrows on his face, and he looked pallid, as if from too little sleep. He was studying the audience, moving from one face to another, assessing. He held up a hand to shield his eyes from the stage lights. And then he found Laura, and locked on. His eyes seemed to blaze at her for a second, then the lids dropped over them. A basilisk stare covered the face she loved.

Laura had expected—what? She did not know. A flash of lightning recognition, perhaps? A kiss transferred across the space between them? Anything but this deadly stare. With a great deal of effort she broke eye contact with him. A shrill laugh focused her to the front row of seats, as Stacey squirmed around in her chair and watched the exchange. Watched, and thoroughly enjoyed it. Laura felt the sharp pain and recognised it: jealousy. It had plagued her every night since he'd left. She had walked painfully through the wreckage as workmen had rebuilt her studio. Her attention to detail had slowed down the run of patients. The only useful thing accomplished had been Rob's portrait. That she had finished, crafting it with all the skill and cunning she possessed.

The chairman banged his gavel, and began going through an agenda like a freight train running out of control. 'Item Number one, treasurer's report. Motion to accept? Vote. Accepted.' Bang, bang as the gavel cracked. It went on and on, lulling Laura into a false sense of security. She had come for one item, and one only. Her mind drifted. Emerald and Belle, left behind on Saba to clean up the house, arrange for shipments, acquaint the new doctor and his wife with the neighbours. In a week, they too would be coming north, ending the idyll of sun and Saba. She would miss it all. *They* would miss it all. And, apart from cleaning the house in Hempstead, Laura had done nothing practical about re-establishing them in a new home.

It would not be Hempstead, she knew. It was too close to New York. Too close to Rob Carlton. The New York papers would be full of his marriage, when it happened, and Laura wanted to be somewhere so small that the local papers would not waste space on a socialite wedding. That far. Like the old joke her grandfather loved to tell: the fisherman, sick of his way of life, put an oar over his shoulder and walked away from the sea. 'The first town I reach where someone says to me, "What's that you're carrying?"'—that's the place where I'm going to settle,' he said. And that was exactly Laura's feeling on the matter. Nothing had been selected yet, but the search committee of the American Dental Association was running through its computer.

Three bangs of the gavel. The extra noise caught Laura's wandering attention and she shifted in her chair. 'Motion submitted by the chief operating officer,' the chairman said. 'Resolved, that the Corporation cancel all plans for the distribution and sale of the Little Mother doll. Vote?'

'Just a minute!' Laura struggled to her feet and glared. Everyone in the room turned to look. 'What happened to the discussion business?' she insisted.

The chairman looked over the top of his glasses at her. 'I don't feel a need to have discussion on this subject,' he said balefully. 'And only stockholders are allowed in this meeting, young lady. Officer, will you escort the lady out?'

There was a security officer standing at the back door. He moved down the aisle in her direction.

'I happen to be a stockholder,' Laura said firmly. She held her stock certificate up over her head. The security officer reached her side and examined the paper.

'It's authentic, sir,' he called back to the chairman. 'One share of stock in the name of Laura Lackland.'

'All right,' the chairman grumbled as he checked on his watch. 'We don't have a great deal of time. What do you want to discuss?'

Laura pulled out her notebook. 'Is it true that this doll's features are painted with a poison—to be specific, lead paint?'

Heads snapped around at the table on the stage. Most of the directors had been relaxed, uncaring. Now they leaned forward across the table, tense. 'Where did you get that information?' the chairman demanded.

'Where isn't important,' Laura maintained stoutly. '*What* is the thing that's important. I have sampling reports from a very prestigious laboratory. And, if I don't get satisfaction here, my next stop will be a briefing for news reporters.'

The gavel banged for several minutes, attempted to quiet a suddenly active crowd. 'Part of your question is correct,' the chairman said gruffly. 'Some of the dolls have been painted with lead paint.'

'Which ones?'

'That's the problem,' Rob Carlton interrupted. 'We don't know which of the two hundred thousand are contaminated.'

'That will be enough!' snapped the chairman, banging his gavel again. 'Do you have any other questions, young lady?'

'Just one.' Laura shouted over the chatter, to be sure she was heard. 'Is it true that *most* of these dolls are stuffed with waste cotton instead of sterilised new cotton?'

The gavel beat a dozen times or more before quiet was restored. 'I don't care to answer that question,' the chairman snarled. 'We will now vote by show of hands.'

'Objection!' Laura shouted. Again the crowd noises, the banging gavel. 'According to the by-laws, a single objection requires a vote by each shareholder, according to the number of shares possessed. I demand such a vote!'

The board went into a huddle, punctuated by a great deal of argument and arm-waving. Eventually they resumed their seats, all glaring grimly at the girl at the back of the room.

'The secretary will conduct the vote,' the chairman droned. There were sixty-two shareholders in the room, including the members of the board. The secretary called them one at a time, registered their vote, and the number of their shares. Only Rob Carlton voted *for* the measure. The totals were posted on a blackboard as each member cast his selection. Being at the back of the room, Laura was the last to be called.

The members of the Board were grinning at each other. Rob examined the tally of votes with an uninterested, tired look. The totals so far indicated sixty-eight thousand *for*, being the total of all his private stock possessions, and seventy-six thousand *against*. Across the long directors' table his brother-in-law, watching the numbers mount, had just cast the proxy vote of his sister, ten thousand shares, *against*. Somehow, Rob had expected it. His sister was so firmly under her husband's thumb that she barely made a move without his permission. And yet it grated on him that the only member of his immediate family would not support him. And so the long hard grind was over, he told himself. There's no need for Laura to cast the final votes. Lovely golden Laura. Rob shrugged his shoulders. He was not the sort of man to look over his shoulder; the future was always in front of him. He listened, very detached, as the secretary stood up.

'And you, Miss Lackland? For what it's worth, where do you cast your one vote? Aye or Nay?'

There was a titter of laughter from the crowd. Stacey Mantoff was the leader of the cheering section. Rob looked blankly across the hall, no longer affected by the decision.

'I cast my one vote Aye,' Laura called. The crowd applauded. A jeer or two interrupted. Rob's head had swivelled around in Laura's direction.

There was a faint tinge of hope on his face. The gavel fell twice. 'Thank you, Miss Lackland, for having wasted half an hour of our time.'

'I'm not finished yet,' Laura said firmly. Another silence fell on the audience. The chairman flushed. The secretary, who maintained the list of authorised voters, smiled. He had been selected by Rob's father, in those long-ago days when Carltons ran Carltonworld.

'Well then, get on with it. I've wasted enough time on this subject today.' The chairman was disgruntled, puzzled, and very angry.

'Perhaps you need a long vacation,' Laura said softly. And then, in a voice loud enough to be heard among the chatter, 'And then I vote the proxy of Miss Emerald Blake Lackland, forty-three thousand, five hundred shares, and the vote is Aye!'

Robert Carlton's office was in the far corner of the thirty-eighth floor, with a view southward, over the rest of Manhattan Island. Laura paced the luxurious room a couple of times. The furniture was chrome American, with about as much taste as cardboard, she told herself. But, since it was none of her business, she turned to the windows, trying to pick out landmarks. The snow was gradually coming to an end. Traffic was moving, albeit slowly, along the city streets, and a plough or two could be seen working their way up Park Avenue.

The door opened behind her, and Robert came in. He looked tired but jaunty, as if the stockholders' meeting had refreshed him. His step bounced, and he tried one of his best smiles on her. I ought to be immune, she thought, but there was still that attraction, which she had to fight.

'Hello, Laura,' he said, coming across the room with arms outstretched. She backed away from him. He slowed to a halt, and his arms dropped, reluctantly.

'Your Mrs Saitemore said you had something important to say. She's a lovely person.'

'Yes,' he agreed. 'She actually runs the firm. I just sit and sign papers.'

'I find that hard to believe. Please say what you have to, Robert, I'm running late. I have to catch a train.'

'I thought you might stay over, Laura.' There was that undefinable ache of longing in his voice, on his face.

'W-whatever gave you that idea?' He's a hard man to refuse, she told herself, so put on the brakes, Dr Lackland. There's no place in your uncomplicated life for Rob Carlton.

'Well, for one thing, you came. I never thought you would. And, for the second thing, you voted for me. Which led me to believe——'

'Look, Mr Carlton.' She did her best to muster up the cold and blustery weather and mix it into her voice. 'Don't believe things you can't see. I came, yes. I voted for you, yes. I did it because, after consultation with my lawyers and some old friends on the Street, I've come to believe you're the best man available to run this corporation. I did it because Emerald's future is involved in your present success.'

Her knees were shaky. To avoid his recognition of the fact, Laura dropped into one of the chairs. It accepted her weight under protest.

'And that was your only reason, Laura?'

'My only reason.'

Rob pulled up another similar chair and sat down facing her. His chair made no protest, no noise. Even the furniture thinks he's a superior being, she told herself glumly. There was a silence that lasted thirty seconds, but felt like thirty years. She decided to break it boldly.

'How's Miss Mantoff? I saw her at the meeting but had no time for talk.'

'Yes, she told me about that. She felt, somehow, that you were trying to insult her. That's naughty, Laura, engaging in intellectual war with Stacey.'

'Yes, I suppose it was,' Laura returned, managing to suppress the little grin that threatened. 'Not fair, I suppose. In intellectual combat, your lovely lady is totally unarmed.'

'And she said something about jealousy and brown belts in karate. You can't claim that as intellectual.'

'So everyone is entitled to their little deceptions, Mr Carlton. Would you get to the point?'

'Yes,' he said. He fiddled with his tie, and Laura restrained the inane urge to jump up and get it straight for him. Say it! she screamed silently. Say whatever it is quickly, and let me go! Just the sight of you is too much!

'OK, I'll get right to the point. Laura, I love you.'

'You'll forgive me if I don't believe you. The game is over, Robert. You have your Carltonworld firmly in your hand. You have Stacey Mantoff to take care of those lonely nights. You don't have to pretend any more. I know my place, and it's not up here on the thirty-eighth floor, nor is it among the sharks you swim with. No, I just don't believe you. You just stick on your side of the world, Robert, and leave me on mine. We'll both be happier.'

'You don't really believe that, Laura—you know you don't. I can tell. Even from this distance, I can tell your body aches for me. Why confuse each other?'

Laura jumped to her feet as he slowly rose. Her face was red. It's the great height, she told herself. And the lack of oxygen. The excuse sounded flimsy, even to herself.

'I never said I didn't want you, Rob. All I said was that I wouldn't *have* you, not under the circumstances we live in.'

'So what do you want me to do?' he asked grimly. 'Give up all I've ever fought for? Turn Carltonworld over to that bunch of vultures? That's too much to ask.' He pounded one fist into the palm of the other and took a few quick paces backwards and forwards.

'Perhaps, Robert. I make no demands on you. Even without your Corporation, I'm not sure we could weather a week together. Maybe—maybe, some day, as a memory of what we might have had, you'll have your Corporation make me a doll like the one I had as a child. I could keep a gift like that, and treasure it. But no, I don't want you to give up your life——'

'You just want me to keep out of yours?'

'I—suppose that's a reasonable summary. I could have loved you in my own way, Robert.'

'Cynara,' he drawled.

'What?'

'It goes, "I have been faithful to thee, Cynara, in my fashion."'

'Oh. See what we dentists never did learn?' Laura fumbled with her wristwatch. 'Oh dear, I'm going to be late if I don't run. There's one thing I do want from you, Robert.'

'Anything,' he promised gruffly. 'What?'

'This.' She threw her arms around his neck and pulled his head down to where she could reach. It was meant to be a tender caress, a loving farewell, but he could not follow the script. Before she could escape, his arms came around her, his lips returned, his shadow engulfed her. Warning bells rang madly in her head; she paid them no attention. Her whole being was crowded narrowly in this attempt to merge herself into him, to make them one in deed and word. The fires flashed up and down her spine. Her cheek burned where his hand came up to touch it. She came up on both toes in her striving, and when he gently set her aside she felt bereft.

'I'll treasure that,' she whispered as she backed away from him in the general direction of the door. Her knees were definitely not co-operating. 'Goodbye, Robert.'

His stern and unrelenting face smouldered. Laura could see the gleam of hidden fires through the dark mist of his eyes. Behind her, the doorknob dug into the small of her back, and she reached behind her and turned it.

'It's not goodbye, Laura. Not yet.'

'It's no use, Robert,' she said firmly. 'I won't even tell you where we're going to live.'

'I'll find you,' he promised. 'Never fear.'

'Dear God, you don't need me. You've got Stacey, and a thousand others. Please don't harass me!'

'I won't. And don't wish people like Stacey on me. I know what I want, Laura, and you're it.'

She could feel the raw essence of him closing the space between them, without him moving a single inch. And then that smile flashed. Before he captured her with his eyes, before she succumbed like any eighteen-year-old fool, Laura Lackland snatched the door open and ran down the hall as if all the hounds of hell were after her. And took the express elevator down!

# CHAPTER ELEVEN

IT WAS not surprising that Laura chose another island for their new home: Martha's Vineyard, nestled under the hook of Cape Cod. There was an advantage. Dr Hiram Friend had a large practice in the town of Oak Bluffs, and needed a three-month break for an operation. It made a nice change for Laura, filling in temporarily. The office was open Monday, Tuesday, a half-day Wednesday, and a full Thursday and Friday.

'You gonna take up golf on Wednesday?' Belle asked suspiciously during the unpacking phase. 'Be like all the rest of them doctors?'

'I don't think so,' Laura chuckled. 'I'll be much too busy. There'll be a million things I need to catch up on.'

'The thing you *really* need, you left behind you somewheres,' the old lady muttered.

'Please, Belle. I want to forget.'

'Wantin' ain't gettin', Missy.'

Wanting a change of subject, Laura started for the stairs. 'I have to take another look upstairs at the roof,' she announced.

'Now what the matter?' growled Belle. 'I say you, don't *buy* a house, rent. Maybe we don't like this place. Don't even have a swimming pool. Big house, about ready to fall down! You think the roof leaks?'

'Just a tiny bit,' Laura sighed. 'I think there was more to that lovable old Yankee real estate man than I thought. You know, you ought to be happier about this, Belle. It's patriotic to own a house. I own one twentieth of it, and the Shawmut Bank owns the rest. After twenty years

I'll own it all. Lord knows where we'll be in twenty years—but I'm sure we'll be rich, and this can be our summer home. And we don't need a swimming pool—dear lord, the Atlantic Ocean is right out there, and there are miles of beaches.'

'It get as cold here like it was in Boston, when we go to school there. How you swim Atlantic Ocean in the winter time, Missy?'

'Well, I'm *not* going to let you discourage me. And I *am* going to check for a roof leak. Isn't it fun to live in such a big old house?'

'Sure.' Belle added, 'If we get the roof fixed, and the plumbing ain't gonna jam up, and the furnace works. You check to see the furnace works?'

'Oh, Belle!' groaned Laura. She had fallen in love with the house as soon as she saw it. Oak Bluffs, like several other seaside towns in Massachusetts, owed its existence to the great religious revival of the 1890s. Evangelical churches held revival meetings that lasted all summer long. Long, hot days were spent with 'fire and brimstone' preachers, long evenings in the enjoyment of God's good world. At first, the church and its parishioners used tents, but gradually the tents were replaced by wooden buildings, until the whole idea of 'camp meeting' became a permanent installation. And because it was the architecture of the time, most of the houses were solid squares with large porches, big airy rooms, not too much plumbing, and a thousand and one ornaments on porch and windows and roofs to which the name 'Gingerbread Gothic' came to be applied. Laura had found just such a house on Elmwood Avenue, barely four blocks away from the circular Church Avenue, once the centre of life in the days of the camp meetings.

It had two other advantages, this house of hers. It was within walking distance of her shared offices, and on the direct school bus route, with a stop directly in front of the house.

Rather than face more of Belle's grumpiness, Laura ran up the narrow stairs to the floor above. The roof *did* leak; she knew that for sure because the leak was right over the middle of her own bed. But today the sun was shining—a warm June sun, tempered by the constant sea breeze that swept the island. Behind the closed door of her own little sanctuary the smile faded quickly. She threw herself down on the bed, face-down, and immediately *he* intruded, crowded out all other thoughts, and brought back all the traitorous feelings of an undisciplined body.

'Damn the man,' she said for the ten thousandth time. 'Either come for me or get out of my head!' She rolled over. The sun was directly over the house, and she could see a penny's worth of light right in the middle of her ceiling. Another of Grandpa's sayings came to mind: I don't need to fix the roof if it isn't raining, and if it *is* raining, the weather's too *bad* for roof work. The thought teased a little smile to her lips. She heaved herself up, smoothed down her dress, and went back downstairs to be with her family.

Laura's first two weeks back at work were tiring. There was new equipment to master, and a couple of new techniques. Patients questioned, unlike the Sabians. They also paid; her income had quadrupled overnight. She walked home slowly on Wednesday noon, determined this time to call the roofers without delay. It was one of those in-between days, with storm clouds to the west, big heavy thunderheads that must be raising havoc on the mainland, and sooner or later might wander out to the island. Belle was in a more cheerful frame of mind. She had come to accept the house, leaks and all, and had made a few friends in the immediate neighbourhood.

'You eat you lunch, Missy, and then you gotta call you answering service. They call for you twice already. Nobody answer in the office——'

'No, everybody's off. Maybe I'd better——'

'Maybe you better eat. And don't hide that milk. You lost fifteen pounds or more in the last few months.'

It wasn't worth an argument. Laura sat down at the table and began on the hot soup. Maybe I have lost weight, she thought. I last saw him in February, and now it's June. If he appeared at the door I'd welcome him, even if he brought Stacey with him. But no, that can't be, can it? How can you be jealous if you're not in love? Or maybe it's just some bug. 'I'll get an appointment with a doctor some day soon, Belle,' she promised. 'We need to find a family physician for all of us.'

'That's a good idea. You like that ham sandwich?'

'Is that what it is? I thought——' Oh lord, Belle is trying to be sweet, she thought, and I'm about to insult her! It all tastes like cardboard! 'Yes, it's fine, and I've eaten it all. Now let me call the answering service.'

'Right after you finish you milk!'

Laura shook her head ruefully, and took the half-empty glass with her into the living-room. The answering service actually responded on the third ring. 'There's a call for emergency service, Dr Lackland,' the thin little voice said. 'A Mr Tribble, who says he's in violent pain, and can't wait. An off-island man.'

'Well——' She thought for a minute, then, 'Where is he?'

'He's waiting outside your office, Doctor. He called on one of those car telephones and left me his number.'

'All right. Call him and tell him I'll be back at the office in ten minutes.'

Laura took the time to wash her face and hands and rearrange her hair. It had grown stringy and lost its

highlights over the winter months. And rebellious. 'I have
an emergency call, Belle,' she called as she headed for
the door. 'I have no idea how long it will take. Look
after Emerald when she gets home from school, please.'

She didn't wait for an answer. Pain was a human state
that need not always be endured. It gave her a sort of
lift, knowing that if she hurried she might save this man
a little pain. The wind was picking up as she strode down
the street, playing with the hem of her dress, snatching
at her hair. The seagulls must have seen the storm
coming, for they had all flown in off the harbour waters
and were squabbling over space on the flat roofs of two
nearby buildings. There was a freshness in the air. Down
the road, parked opposite her office, was a heavy sedan
with Massachusetts number plates. Laura beckoned to
the occupant as she climbed the stairs and unlocked the
front door.

He must have come at once. His footsteps echoed
behind her on the polished floor. She went directly to
the treatment room without stopping to look back,
checked her instruments, and gestured towards the chair.
'If you'll just have a seat, Mr Tribble, I'll be—oh no!
You!' When she turned around, grinning up at her was
Robert Carlton.

'Yeth, me,' he mumbled. The side of his face was
swollen.

'What are you *doing* here?' she demanded, her voice
going shrill in panic.

He shrugged and pointed towards his swollen cheek.
Laura looked down. Her hands were trembling as if from
ague. Even her teeth chattered. She turned away from
him for a moment to regain her control. After all these
weeks, to meet again like this! How could he know where
she was? But he must be in pain, and with that swelling.
She took a deep breath to steady her nerves, picked up
mirror and pick, and turned back to him.

'All right, Mr Carlton. Open your mouth, please.' She snapped on her directional light and leaned over to look into the cavern of his mouth.

'Why, you——!' It wasn't ladylike at all, what she said next. She slammed her pick down on the tray, picked up her forceps, and pulled out of his *swollen* cheek an extra large chocolate. 'Of all the rotten——'

'Ah, that feels much better.' That famous smile was spread across his wide, gentle face. Gentle? Where did I get that word? she fumed. It disturbed her, irritated her, charmed her.

'What—what do you think you're doing?' It was almost impossible to be angry, because she was so glad to see him again. 'I was—I thought you'd never come,' she admitted, flustered. 'Why did you?'

'We have a lot of business to talk over, Laura.'

'But why all this—charade?'

'Because, while the Dental Association was willing to tell me where you worked, they had no idea where you lived,' he chuckled. 'I figured that, since I didn't want to walk every street on the island, I'd have to think up some ploy to bring you here. Worked, didn't it?'

'Lord, you are devious!' she sighed. 'Get up out of there. I charge heavily for people who sit in *that* chair. Back home, I have one where you can sit for free.'

'Sounds nice to me,' Rob agreed, unfolding from the contoured chair. 'But I need a little something to go on.'

'What's *that* supposed to mean?'

He demonstrated, rather than explained. Short but sweet, the kiss surprised Laura almost as much as his unexpected presence. She had forgotten how sweet a kiss could be. Forgotten why she had turned him out of her house in far-off Saba. Forgotten. And now it all came back.

'Did you come to try to take Emerald away from me?'

Rob flinched at the anger in her voice, then took her by the elbows. 'I never had any intention of taking Emerald away from you, Laura. Never. That was all my brother-in-law's doing. Carltonworld withdrew from the case the day after I returned to New York.'

'You mean that, Robert?' She knew the minute the words were out of her mouth that the question was needless. He was not that sort of man. She could not say *why* she knew, she just did.

'I do.' He took her arm and led her out of the house to his car. 'Rental,' he explained. 'I flew into Boston yesterday, and drove down today.'

'Good heavens! You mean you brought this over on the steamship? They have sixty-day waiting lists! How in the world did——'

'Just lucky, I guess.' He grinned down at her. 'Buckle up, lady. It's the law in this state. Directions, please?'

Laura provided them, fighting off her body's need to grab at him, to hold him close. 'I'm sorry about Stacey,' she offered quietly. Rob swung the car around the corner and parked in front of her house.

'Sorry? Why should you be sorry about Stacey? She hit the jackpot. Don't tell me that you hear all the society gossip up in this little corner of the world?'

Laura ducked her head and reached for the door-handle. Anything to keep him from seeing her face. 'No,' she admitted. 'It's just that—well, to tell the truth, I subscribe to a clipping service. They sent me the wedding story, and things like that. And I'm not sorry for Stacey—I'm sorry for you, Robert.'

His whoop of laughter startled the little corgi who lived next door. The dog ran over to the car, barking madly, with tail wagging just as emphatically.

'What's so funny?' demanded Laura suspiciously.

'You thought Stacey getting married would upset me? That's funny, lady. Stacey's a friend of my *sister's*. I've been trying to get her married off for the past ten years!'

'Oh, my,' she muttered, and sank back deeply into her seat. Another misconception gone west! He didn't try to steal Emerald, and he didn't love Stacey, she thought. Her forehead wrinkled with a deep frown. Then if all that's true, why have we been apart all these months?

'I didn't know,' she mumbled. 'She said something to me once about—about you and her. I thought—would you like to come in?'

'That's what I'm here for,' he chuckled. 'You go ahead. I have a couple of packages I need to bring in. So, you've been keeping up with me all this time?'

'No such thing! I never even gave you a thought!' Laura stepped out of the car and walked proudly up the stairs. Rob followed closely, one hand filled with his packages, the other reaching trustingly for the porch rail.

'No!' she exclaimed in alarm.

He stopped dead in his tracks. 'No? You don't want me to come in?'

'Yes, I want you to come in,' she stammered. 'I just didn't want you to fall down. That rail is full of termites. If the real estate agent from whom I bought this place ever has a toothache, I'm planning to get even!'

'Poor little Laura,' commented Rob in syrupy sympathy as he followed her into the house.

'In here, Robert. This is our living-room. Please sit down. I need to tell Belle that——'

'You don't need tell Belle nothin', Missy. I heard you come up the stairs. You a mean, arrogant man, Robert Carlton, but you good for my Missy. What took you so long?'

He sat down in one of the comfortable old Morris chairs that had come with the house, and smiled up at them both. 'Business,' he said, and refused to amplify.

'Where you stay, man? Don't have any vacancies around this island in the tourist season.'

'I don't have a place yet,' he said. That teasing, wistful smile was back. 'I was hoping——'

'You stay here,' Belle concluded. 'We have supper five o'clock. No omelette, Missy, not tonight. We have steak! I go get it out.'

'Before you go, Belle, I brought you a present.' Rob stood up to hand her one of the packages. Her eager, strong fingers fumbled with the string.

'Ain't many people bring me presents,' she said as she finally managed the knot.

'Why, Belle, you're crying!' Laura could only remember twice in her life when she had seen the old woman cry. The first had been at her grandfather's funeral, the second on the day that Anne died.

'I ain't cryin',' Belle insisted firmly. 'I jus' got something in the eye. Chocolates! How you know that, man? Who told you Belle likes chocolates?'

'With rum fillings,' he chuckled. 'Emerald told me. Who else in this house is a chatterbox? Better take the box with you. I understand others in the family like them, too.'

'Miss Laura like them, but don't eat them,' Belle said practically. 'Not good for her—break out all over, she does. I gonna go, get the supper, get you a room. Treat him nice, Missy.'

Laura hid her smile and sat down demurely on the sofa next to his chair.

'Haven't given me a thought in all these months, you say?' drawled Rob. She flinched, then folded her hands primly in her lap.

'Not a minute,' she lied.

'I thought that might be so,' he chuckled. 'You're a poor poker player, golden Laura. If you haven't given me a thought, how come mine is the only painting hanging on the wall?' He gestured over to the area between the two front windows. The painting was the unfinished work he had seen on Saba. It showed him leaning back at a table with a brooding look on his face.

'Well——' she fumbled, 'I don't have to answer that. I have rights under the First Amendment of the Constitution!' She bowed her head, swinging her long hair across part of her blushing face.

'We have a lot of making up to do,' he said firmly. 'Ladies first.' Laura took a deep breath and straightened her back.

'You're not in love with Stacey?'

'No. I told you I was in love with you! How dense can one girl be?'

'You haven't a clue yet,' she muttered. 'You and your darn corporation. I can't make it in the league with all those tycoons. I just can't!'

'Neither can I,' he retorted. 'I bought a plant out in Illinois, run by a very savvy man. He's now the chief executive officer of Carltonworld. I'm just a stockholder. Starting in the fall semester I'll be an Associate Professor of Engineering at the University of Rhode Island, right across the bay. That's the second thing I did after I got back from Saba.'

'You—you're not——' Laura grounded both feet flat on the rug and sat up even straighter. 'What was the *first* thing?'

'Womanly curiosity? I'm glad you're not interested in me. The first thing I did was to fire my stupid brother-in-law.'

'And what are you planning until your school opens?'

'I'm planning to get married and raise a family of little dentists,' he said cheerfully. Both Laura's hands came up to her overheated cheeks.

'You mean——?'

'I mean you, dummy!'

'I—oh, Robert!' She was up from the sofa in a flash, depositing herself in his lap. His arms came around her gently and folded her into his broad chest. The comfort was so overwhelming that she began to cry.

'Now what's the matter? I don't usually have that effect on women!'

'I'm crying because I'm so happy,' she sniffed. 'You've given up so much, for such a worthless prize.'

'Don't underrate yourself,' he reminded her. 'You're worth everything I have in the world.'

It was heavenly, lying there, spilling salt tears on his soft blue shirt, but eventually the world intervened. 'I have to—there's Emerald and Belle to consider,' she sighed.

'Belle is no problem,' he mused. 'As far as I'm concerned, she's my mother-in-law.'

'But Emerald *is* a problem?' Her anxiety would not let her rest.

'Not now,' he said. 'At first, down in Saba—I just couldn't adjust to the idea that she was your daughter.'

'But she is,' Laura insisted despondently. 'And always will be. What's the problem?'

'I can't quite explain it,' he sighed. 'Who is her father?'

'We never could find out, Robert.'

'You're her mother and you don't know who her father is?' That cold steel look was back in his eyes. He set her aside, got up, and paced the room a time or two, trying to master his anger. 'I'm not a moralist or a judge, Laura. I couldn't help but wonder. But that's behind us. Emerald is *our* daughter, right?'

'What in the world are you thinking, Robert? Emerald is——'

They were interrupted. The door slammed behind the little girl and she came running into the room. 'Mama——' And then she spotted Rob.

'Rob!' she screeched, and ran across the room to jump at him. He caught her in mid-air, swung her around a time or two, and gave her a big kiss. Laura was close enough to recognise love when she saw it—on both faces. She relaxed and waited. He swung the child around again, then let her feet touch the floor. Instantly, Emerald was across the room to her mother to repeat the performance.

'Mama—you'll be surprised!'

'Yes, I'm sure I will, love. What?'

'We had a special teacher come to the class today to talk about sex education. They split the class up, the boys in one room and the girls in another. And you know what she asked us?'

'No, I haven't the faintest idea,' said Laura, accustomed to these long-winded outbursts of enthusiasm. Over the child's head she could see Rob's grin widen alarmingly.

'She asked us if we knew how babies come!' the child shouted in glee. 'And I was the only one who knew!'

'Oh, my!' Laura blushed. 'You're too heavy for me. Why don't you run out in the kitchen for your snack?'

'Just a minute,' Rob intervened. 'I want to learn something myself. How *do* babies come, Emerald?'

The child looked back at him over her shoulder, the happy intensity of life sparkling out of her eyes. And, perhaps, Laura thought, just a touch of devilishness too.

'That's easy,' called Emerald. 'In a basket, like me!' And she went skipping down the hall, singing.

Laura turned away from the door, bemused. Rob came over to her and shook her by the shoulders, very gently. 'Explain,' he demanded.

'Explain what?' she asked innocently.

'Emerald came in a basket,' he snapped. 'And what else?'

The laughter could not be held back. Laura let it flow, falling back into the chair behind her. After a couple of minutes he passed her a handkerchief. 'Dry your eyes, for God's sake,' he rumbled. 'Emerald?'

'I can't help laughing, Robert. You thought I was her *natural* mother all this time, didn't you? Well, she just told you the truth. Emerald was a foundling, left on our doorstep in a little basket. We still have it upstairs. My sister Anne had been married for some years, and no children had come, and she wanted one. So Grandpa and I took Emerald to the Blakes and they were allowed to adopt her. And then, when she was still a baby, there was that horrible accident. Anne lived for a time; her husband died immediately. She made me promise to raise Emerald myself, to give her all the love she needed. So I adopted her. In Connecticut, that was. Which is why your stupid New York lawyers couldn't find a record of it all.'

'And you've never had a child, Laura?'

'Not a natural child, no. In fact, love, I've never had a man of my own, either.'

'Well, *that's* over,' he said decisively. 'We're going to get married, you and I.' He wasn't exactly asking, and Laura wasn't exactly objecting. He had swung her up into his arms again, and she was finding it difficult to breathe. 'Oh, one more item,' he said. 'I brought *you* a present too.' He set her down carefully on the sofa and put the small box in her lap. She offered her thanks and fumbled with the wrapping paper.

Inside the box, a little tow-headed doll stared back at her with deep green eyes. There was something suspicious about it all, Laura thought, then caught a glimpse of herself in the wall mirror. The doll was made in her exact image!

'Robert!' she squealed. 'It's—it—what does it do?'

'Nothing,' he said solemnly. 'It just lies there and lets you love it, just the way you ordered.'

The outside world seized that moment to interrupt. A long roll of thunder shook the house, and rain beat against the front windows.

'Missy!' Belle shouted from the kitchen. 'I got windows open upstairs and down. You close the ones upward, while I do these down here. And *hurry*! We'll be soaked!'

'We're hurrying!' Rob called back. Laura slipped her arms around his neck as he carried her up the stairs and, purely by luck, into her own bedroom. The big double bed bounced as he dropped her. He closed the windows, then went down the corridor to the other rooms.

Laura gazed around. The room sparkled in the darkness of the storm. The grey rug seemed much brighter, the mirrors shone, the trios of little bluebirds on the wallpaper were actually *singing*. Very carefully but efficiently, she began to unbutton her blouse.

The first cold drop landed right in the middle of Rob's bare back. His head came up from its nest between her breasts.

'You don't think you could try again?' she begged. 'They say third time takes all!'

He collapsed on top of her. 'I don't think I could lick a postage stamp right this minute.'

'Darn,' she laughed. 'You tycoons aren't what you're cracked up to be. Oh, love!' She managed to get her hands around his chest, and touched the water in the hollow of his back. 'I forgot to tell you——' she sighed. 'The roof leaks.'

'Thank God for that,' he chuckled. 'I thought I'd broken a blood vessel. Why are we in such a hurry?'

'Because I'm almost thirty,' said Laura very firmly, nipping at his ear with her sharp little teeth. 'There's a great deal of life I've missed, and I want to catch up. Besides, I don't want to have Emerald grow up as an only child.'

'I see,' he laughed. 'There's a time for sowing, and——'

'And a time for reaping,' she said solemnly. 'Would you rather go fix the roof, or——?'

'No, thanks, sweetheart. I'm getting my strength back slowly. I think a little more sowing is in order. And that's an order!'

'Yes, sir,' she giggled, and grinned at the nose that was barely an inch from her own.

From the head of the stairs, Laura could hear Belle calling. 'Emerald! You get away from those stairs! You mama havin' words with you new papa!'

Laura sighed and wrapped her arms around Rob's neck. 'Well, Mr Carlton,' she whispered in his ear, 'have I tamed you yet?'

'Hey, yes,' he chuckled. 'You've got me right where I want you. Now, let me see, where was I?'

# Harlequin Romance

## Coming Next Month

**2947  BENEATH WIMMERA SKIES  Kerry Allyne**
Mallory is tired of her international jet-set modeling career and
wants only to manage the outback ranch where she grew up.
Unfortunately, Bren Dalton, the man with the say-so, doesn't think
Mallory capable of it.

**2948  SEND ME NO FLOWERS  Katherine Arthur**
Samantha has doubts about ghostwriting Mark Westland's memoirs,
despite the elderly actor's charm. And when it brings Blaize
Leighton to her door, determined to keep his mother's name out of
the book, her life becomes suddenly complicated....

**2949  THE DIAMOND TRAP  Bethany Campbell**
A schoolteacher's life is thrown off balance when she chaperones a
young music prodigy to Nashville—and falls for the very man she
came to protect her student from! And what about her fiancé back
home?

**2950  YOU CAN LOVE A STRANGER  Charlotte Lamb**
Late-night radio disc jockey Maddie enjoys her life in the quiet
seaside town—until Zachary Nash, a stranger with an intriguing
velvety voice, involves her in a tangle of emotional relationships
that turn her life upside down!

**2951  STRICTLY BUSINESS  Leigh Michaels**
Gianna West and Blake Whittaker, friends from childhood, now
senior partners in a cosmetics company, have known each other too
long to cherish romantic notions about each other. Or so Gianna
believes—until a glamorous rival causes a change of mind...and
heart.

**2952  COLOUR THE SKY RED  Annabel Murray**
As a writer of horror stories, Teale Munro works very unsocial
hours, and he assumes Briony, as an artist, will understand why he
feels able to offer her only an affair. Except that he badly misjudges
Briony and her feelings....

Available in December wherever paperback books are sold,
or through Harlequin Reader Service.

In the U.S.                          In Canada
901 Fuhrmann Blvd.                   P.O. Box 603
P.O. Box 1397                        Fort Erie, Ontario
Buffalo, N.Y.  14240-1397            L2A 5X3

# *Harlequin American Romance*

## Romances that go one step farther...
## American Romance

Realistic stories involving people you can relate to and care about.

Compelling relationships between the mature men and women of today's world.

Romances that capture the core of genuine emotions between a man and a woman.

Join us each month for four new titles wherever paperback books are sold.
Enter the world of American Romance.

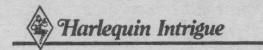

# Harlequin Intrigue

Two exciting new stories each month.

Each title mixes a contemporary, sophisticated romance with the surprising twists and turns of a puzzler... romance with "something more."

Because romance can be quite an adventure.

**Romance, Suspense and Adventure**